Jacob's Ladder

A Journey through Books, Manners, and the Mysteries of Life

By Christopher Richardson

Presentation

Hey there, Awesome Reader!

So, you've stumbled upon this book, huh? Well, grab your favorite drink and get comfy because we're about to embark on a wild journey together! This isn't just any book; it's a kaleidoscope of ideas that I've been cooking up for ages. The inspiration hit me like a freight train when I realized how many untold stories were swirling around us, begging to be released into the world. The spark ignited, and I immediately started scribbling notes on whatever I could find—napkins, my phone, even the back of grocery receipts!

It all started as a passion project, fueled by my desire to connect with others through shared experiences. I delved deep into the research, exploring countless books, articles, and interviews, soaking up every piece of information like a sponge. I even reached out to experts in the field, sharing conversations that would change the course of this book. Each interview and every insightful snippet found its way into the chapters you're about to read. It was like catching lightning bugs in a jar—brilliant ideas captured in the darkness!

As I pieced together the narrative, I realized that what I was creating was not merely a collection of thoughts, but a living, breathing entity filled with potential. The structure began to take shape, evolving through multiple drafts, long nights, and even the occasional existential crisis! I wanted to ensure that every page turned would bring a new revelation, a fresh perspective, or a hearty chuckle. So, I've worked tirelessly to keep the rhythm lively and engaging, interspersing facts with anecdotes that are at once serious yet sprinkled with a touch of humor.

The word count? Off the charts! Yet every word was chosen with care, with the aim of keeping you entertained while stuffing your brain with knowledge. Let's face it: who said learning couldn't be fun? I wanted this book to feel like an exhilarating roller coaster—twists, turns, and all. And while you're screaming out of delight at the unexpected dips, you also gain wisdom on a platter!

I encourage you to read till the very end because trust me, the last chapters will leave you buzzing with excitement. We're diving into questions that don't just skim the surface but dive headfirst into the deep end of the pool—eye-opening stuff coming your way! And you, my dear reader, are right at the center of this mad science experiment we call literature. Think of yourself as a collaborator, an active participant transforming a solitary endeavor into something profoundly collective. It's an invitation to you to laugh, reflect, disagree, or even shout at the pages.

There will be moments that challenge you, pushing the boundaries of how you see the world, and that's the whole point! Together, we're going to explore themes that resonate deeply, ones that keep us up at night thinking. Some may even prick at your heartstrings, and I absolutely embrace that! I hope you keep an open mind and an even wider heart as you dance through these pages. By the time you reach the finish line, I promise you'll be left with more questions than answers—exciting questions!

I want you to feel every emotion—delight, heartbreak, curiosity—because that's what makes storytelling a powerful force. After all, isn't it the unexpected twists that keep you on the edge of your seat? This journey might feel like a rollercoaster, but buckle up, hold on tight, and get ready for the ride of your life! The adventure has just begun, and I couldn't be more thrilled to have you along with me. So, are you ready? Let's dive into the pages ahead and uncover the magic waiting just for you!

With excitement in every word.

Christopher Richardson.

Table of Contents

The Whispering Aisles

Entering the Library

As the heavy wooden doors creaked open, Adam took a tentative step inside the library, and it was as if he had crossed into another world. The air shimmered with the scent of aged paper and dust, mingling with the faint aroma of polished wood. An almost palpable energy surrounded him, thick with mystery and wonder. This expansive sanctuary was a realm where time seemed to stretch, caught between the pages of the countless tomes that towered all around.

Adam's heart raced with a blend of excitement and awe as he gazed up at the lofty shelves that loomed overhead. Each shelf was groaning under the weight of its heavy burdens—books of every size, shape, and color. Some were leather-bound, their spines embossed with gilded lettering, while others were tattered and frayed, their histories written not just in words but in the scars of wear and time. Every book appeared to whisper secrets of adventures long forgotten, tales yearning to be told anew.

As he ventured deeper into the library's embrace, the soft lighting cast a warm glow over the countless volumes, illuminating the dust motes swirling lazily in the air. Shadows danced upon the walls, creating ethereal shapes that flickered and changed at the corners of his vision. Adam's imagination took flight; those shapes seemed to pulse and sway, telling stories that nobody else could hear. He felt as if the library itself was alive, breathing with the essence of creativity and possibility.

An invisible thread tugged at Adam's heart, pulling him further into the labyrinthine aisles. He navigated between rows of books, the wooden floor creaking softly beneath him, almost as if echoing the very steps of the literary giants who once wandered these realms. Here was a space untouched by the hustle and bustle of the outside world, where curiosity reigned supreme, and the adventures of the mind took precedence.

With every step, he felt a deepening sense of destiny, as if he were meant to uncover the treasures hidden between the covers of the books surrounding him. He reached out, brushing his fingers across the spines, each touch igniting a spark of wonder. Old encyclopedias, encyclopedic tomes of knowledge, beckoned enticingly, while others promised escapades into fantastical worlds too magnificent to exist in the ordinary realm. Adam sensed that something extraordinary lay just beyond his grasp—a door waiting to be opened, a path waiting to be explored.

His imagination began to spin stories of his own—of knights and dragons, of distant galaxies and undiscovered lands. He envisioned himself as a character in one of those stories, emboldened by the magic of the library. What if he stumbled upon a tome that contained secrets about the universe? What if he uncovered a manuscript that held the thoughts of poets from centuries past?

As he moved through the aisles, he noticed how the layout of the library resembled a great maze. The towering shelves were like sentinels, standing guard over the literary realm, while narrow pathways wove in and out of the rows. The overhead lights created an aura of enchantment, illuminating the way ahead while casting mysterious shadows behind him.

It was as if the walls themselves were whispering guidance, encouraging him to explore further.

For Adam, every book was a promise. Each volume whispered of sprawling voyages and heroic feats while evoking the heart's yearning for discovery. He felt the stirrings of a thousand stories brush against his consciousness, teasing him with fragments of dreams left unfulfilled. Who had written these books? What inspired their thoughts? Did the authors feel the same surge of curiosity that now coursed through him?

As he turned the corner of an aisle, he came to a stop. Before him stood a collection of books with ornate covers and intricate designs—volumes that appeared almost regal in their presentation. he stepped closer, and his heart fluttered with anticipation. One book, in particular, drew him in with its vibrant colors and shimmering gold leaf. The title, embossed in exquisite script, promised adventures that could only exist between the pages.

As Adam reached for it, he felt the thrill of a discovery waiting to happen. His fingers brushed against the spine, the texture of the cover sending a ripple of excitement through him. Just as he was about to pull it from the shelf, a fleeting movement caught his eye—something scuttled across the floor, drawing his attention away from the enticing tome.

He knelt down to get a better look, and there it was: a cockroach, but not an ordinary one. This creature sparkled, its shell glimmering as if dusted with silver. Adam felt a rush of enticement mixed with disbelief. It paused briefly to regard him with beady eyes before darting forward, disappearing into the shadows of the aisle.

Intrigued, Adam jumped to his feet and chased after it. He felt a surge of energy as he followed this peculiar guide, weaving through the narrow gaps between towering shelves, past currents of dust that sparkled like stars in the dim light. The library felt both expansive and intimate, a cosmos within itself filled with palpable spirit and potential. The cockroach led him further away from the familiar sections, into a nook that felt shrouded in mystery.

The shadows danced more energetically here, casting familiar shapes that beckoned him forward. Adam allowed curiosity to take the lead, letting the cockroach lead him deeper into the depths of the library. He felt exhilarated, ready to plunge headfirst into the unknown. This room seemed to whisper promises of forgotten tales and hidden wisdom—an eerie yet inviting allure.

Suddenly, Adam stopped short. The cockroach had vanished around a corner, and he found himself at the mouth of a new aisle—a passageway filled with the slightest hint of adventure, a darkened corridor that felt charged with untold stories. He took a deep breath, brimming with anticipation. He reached out to grab the nearest book and felt its weight in his hands, the anticipation coursing through him like electricity.

The library had transformed him already; he was no longer just a boy chasing an anomaly but a seeker of knowledge and adventure. Nothing felt out of reach in this sanctuary of learning.

As he stepped further into the unknown, the walls whispered louder, urging him onward, igniting sparks of creativity and enticing dreams of possibility. With hearts full of curiosity, Adam and the library embarked on a journey that would forge bonds between past and future, imagination and reality. It was a journey that would not only change Adam but would connect him to the facets of life that lay hidden within the folds of every story.

The Call of Knowledge

In the heart of the library, where dust motes danced in the golden light filtering through stained glass windows, Adam felt a stirring within him that transcended mere curiosity. It was as if the very walls of the library hummed with a silent energy, creating a symphony of whispers urging him to delve deeper into the unknown. Each bookshelf, lined with tomes that seemed to stretch infinitely into the ether, held a story that awaited him, and he was drawn to them like a moth to a flame. This was not just a collection of books arranged systematically; it was a treasure trove of knowledge, containing secrets both mundane and mystical, shaped by the hands of countless authors who had poured their souls into each page.

As he wandered the aisles, memories of bedtime stories with his father, Bobby, enveloped him like a warm blanket. He could still hear his father's voice resonating through the years, weaving enchanting tales that transported them to distant lands filled with magnificent creatures and daring heroes. It was in those moments, wrapped snugly in the warmth of familiarity, that Adam found his imagination stretched to its limits, urging him to dream wider and deeper.

His father had always expounded on the importance of knowledge, emphasizing how each book was a doorway to new adventures, new perspectives, and new ideas. Bobby's own artistic journey, punctuated by struggles and triumphs, guided Adam's understanding of literature as not just words bound in paper, but as bridges to empathy and understanding. The stories shared often sparked questions in Adam's young mind, igniting a yearning to explore more than just his immediate surroundings. Now, standing amidst the towering shelves, he could almost hear Bobby's voice echoing in his heart, beckoning him to discover what lay beyond the polished wood and leather bindings.

The library's scent, a rich bouquet of aged leather and musty paper, enveloped him, awakening sensations that felt both familiar and new. It ignited within Adam a longing so profound that it felt like an unquenchable thirst. He inhaled deeply, letting the fragrance of history and wisdom infuse his very being. It reminded him of quiet afternoons spent with Bobby, flipping through colorful picture books, immersing himself in illustrations that came alive under their fingers. Now, each turn of the page in this vast temple of knowledge resonated with the promise of discovery.

With each step he took, the floor creaked softly beneath him, reinforcing the sense of stepping into a world carved out by generations who had walked the same path, tracing the lineage of thought and artistry. No longer was he merely a visitor, a quiet child wandering lost among the stacks; he was an active participant in a grand narrative, awakening the adventurer within. As his fingers lightly brushed against the spines of the books that formed a winding path around him, he imagined them as his guides, ready to lead him through unimaginable realms. In that moment, he understood that the library wasn't just a place of stillness; it was a vast ocean of stories, each book a vessel waiting to be explored.

The first book he picked seemed to hum softly beneath his fingers, an inviting warmth emanating from its cover. Turning it slowly, he marveled at its age, the worn-out corners whispering secrets of its past journeys. The title, barely legible, hinted at an adventure that had traveled through time and space, waiting for a kindred spirit to lift it from its slumber. Adam's excitement surged, pushing aside any worries or uncertainties. He was ready to uncover what lay within these pages, to understand not only the tales told but also the lessons wrapped within them.

It was as if the library itself guided him towards the stories that called to his heart. Time slipped away, and the outside world faded into a mere backdrop, replaced by the universe of imagination opened up just for him. He remembered snippets of wisdom his father had shared, reinforcing the idea that each story he encountered would serve as a mirror, reflecting not just the world around him but also the world within. Adam's mind raced with possibilities as he embraced this newfound sense of agency, empowered to delve deeper and ask questions that once felt too large for his small frame.

As his journey through the aisles continued, familiar titles popped out in bursts of color, igniting memories of the adventures Bobby had brought to life so passionately. He lost himself in thoughts of heroes overcoming great odds, friendships blossoming, and lessons on kindness—tales that echoed with the core of humanity, stirring a desire in him to contribute his own voice to such captivating narratives. Each book represented a path lined with potential; it was exhilarating to think that he would one day write his own stories, ones that could inspire others just as he had been inspired.

From the corner of his eye, he noticed titles written in different scripts and styles. Each language pulled at his heartstrings, reminding him of the world outside the library's confines. The idea of different cultures, each with its unique stories, unleashed a wave of curiosity. What tales might they tell? What lessons did they hold that could expand the boundaries of his understanding? He felt the urge to delve into these tales as well, to connect with voices from far-off lands and ancient traditions woven into the fabric of existence.

The soft rustle of the pages around him played like a soothing symphony in the background, and for the first time, Adam sensed the rhythmic connection shared among the stories. They whispered tales of love, sorrow, adventure, and discovery, threading together the lifelines of predecessors who had pondered the same questions he had just begun to explore. The momentum of these whispers amplified his excitement, converting his childhood wonder into a fierce appetite for knowledge and adventure.

Yet, beyond the curiosity simmering within him, there was a growing awareness of his father's life beyond this sanctuary of learning. In his mind's eye, he pictured Bobby painting in their small apartment, splattering colors with both determination and hesitation. Adam wished to recall the stories he had told about the struggles in translating visions into masterpieces, how he sometimes felt lost amidst canvases that reflected his unfulfilled dreams.

In that moment, Adam felt a deep yearning to intertwine both their journeys. He wanted to be the bridge that connected Bobby's world of paint and canvas with the pages of the stories resonating in this library. The tales within these old volumes held the power to inspire his father's artistry just as they had inspired him. Underneath the layers of adventure and fantasy lay fundamental truths about the human experience; those stories could illuminate the creative spirit that once flowed so freely through Bobby's veins.

With a heart full of purpose, Adam picked up books, one after another, immersing himself in the tales while questioning how each lesson could be translated into lived experience. As he poured through stories, he began to weave them into the fabric of his own developing voice. Every tale offered guidance; a lesson he hoped to share with Bobby and the encounters they had yet to experience together.

Suddenly, as Adam absorbed knowledge from various cultures, he recognized the quiet power residing in kindness and understanding—qualities that echoed through every corner of the library. The whimsical fantasy worlds transported him momentarily, but the realities within those stories mirrored the concerns that loomed in his home life. Adam realized that he could harness the lessons learned from these narratives to approach Bobby with newfound compassion and empathy.

In the midst of this literary adventure, Adam couldn't shake the feeling that he wasn't merely learning for himself anymore; this was an opportunity to become the keeper of stories that could infuse both their lives with meaning. He envisioned sitting next to his father, both immersed in reading, discussing the plots, and bringing to life the characters that danced across the page. Together, they would explore ideas on how kindness could transform lives, how exploring fears could lead to understanding oneself, and how art and literature could meld harmoniously in their journey forward.

His heart brimming with hope, Adam sought to harness that possibility into a tangible goal. The library had awakened something within him—a thirst not just for stories, but for connection and growth. With every page turned, he lit a spark of inspiration in his soul, one that promised to shine like the sun. His curiosity blossomed into a yearning for shared experience, something beyond individual narratives.

As shadows began to stretch across the library floor, replicating the sense of timelessness that the books had offered him, he knew his adventure was only the beginning. The call of knowledge echoed around him, binding him to a world ripe for exploration and discovery. Each whisper resounded in his heart, igniting a flame of passion that would carry them through the complexities of life together.

And so, the library stretched and expanded before him—a universe of stories laden with treasures. Adam felt himself not just standing in the presence of knowledge but also stepping into a legacy that intertwined with the very essence of who he and Bobby were destined to become: storytellers, creators, and above all, explorers navigating the profound waters of existence. The journey ahead shimmered with promise as the call of knowledge led him into the adventures that beckoned, standing on the precipice of a new chapter unfolding in their shared narrative.

The Cockroach Appears

In the hushed ambiance of the library, where dust motes floated lazily in slants of golden light, Adam wandered beyond the ordinary. It was a world poised between reality and the fantastical. The sound of his small footsteps echoed softly against the wooden floor, merging with the whispers of ancient texts tucked away on worn shelves. The air was thick with stories begging to be told, secrets eager to escape their bindings.

As he meandered through the labyrinth of literature, each aisle felt like a passage through time—a people's history bound in pages and ink. Leather-bound tomes lay sedimented in quiet corners while encyclopedias stood tall, like sentinels guarding the knowledge amassed over centuries. For a moment, Adam felt the weight of possibility, the universe opening up before him, ready to share its endless wonders.

But it was then that a glimmer caught his eye, something unusual skimming over the surface of reality. A flash of movement, quick and unexpected, darted past him: a cockroach, gleaming as if it wore a coat of silver. It moved nimbly and gracefully, weaving through the shadows, as though it belonged to another realm altogether. Adam felt a sudden jolt of intrigue, a flicker of adventure igniting within him.

Curiosity propelled him forward, his feet rising from the ground, following the creature into the unknown. The sound of the cockroach's legs tapping against the floor resonated like a heartbeat, and he felt an undeniable pull, a connection urging him to discover where this shimmering entity might lead him.

With an upturned brow and a heart of wonder, Adam pursued the flickering flash of silver, every scurry marking a moment of serendipity. He turned corners that led him deeper into the library, toward areas he had previously overlooked— well beyond the sunny sections filled with whimsical fairy tales or heroic sagas—into a quieter realm where the golden glow began to fade into shadow.

Every twist and turn brought a renewed sense of excitement bubbling in his chest. The air thickened with an unfamiliar essence, tinged with the scent of aged paper and lingering secrets. Dust swirled around him, dancing in the dim light, urging him to breathe deeply and embrace the magic of the moment.

Through a narrow gap between towering bookcases draped in cobwebs, Adam glimpsed the cockroach disappearing into an alcove, a hidden nook that seemed to beckon him closer. As he squeezed between the shelves, the world felt like it shifted slightly—sound muffled, light dimmed, and everything seemed tinged with a dreamlike quality that made him question whether he was still in the library or if he had crossed over into another dimension.

Stepping into the nook, he was greeted by the sight of ancient manuscripts and forgotten journals that lay scattered across a dusty table. The cockroach paused at the center of it all, turning to look back at him as though waiting to see what he would do next. Adam felt a surge of spontaneity awaken within him; his apprehensions melted away, replaced with an audacity to explore the peculiarities before him.

The table bore the weight of history; crumbling pages hinted at stories long forgotten, and ink stains told tales of dreams once etched with fervor. Adam moved closer, his tiny fingers brushing over the spines of various tomes. Each title played a melody in his mind, strumming chords of recollection from tales his father had shared—of kings and queens, of courage and compassion. Yet here, among these dusty relics, was the promise of exploration that felt different, unrestrained by the bounds of familiarity.

The cockroach scurried sideways, emboldening Adam to lean further into the adventure.

"What hides in your secrets?" he whispered, almost reverently, half-expecting a reply.

In that moment, the cockroach seemed to shimmer even brighter, as if responding in its own way. Encouraged, Adam decided to dive into the mystery the nook provided. One book caught his eye, tattered and yet beautiful, an enigma waiting for someone to unravel its layers.

With careful thoughts racing, Adam reached out, fingers trembling slightly as they grasped the worn cover. The moment he opened it, a rush of air swept through the space, making the hairs on his arms stand on end. The pages fluttered like wings trying to escape, each one momentarily alive with potential before settling softly under the weight of his small hand. The words seemed to sparkle, resonating with energy that vibrated against the fragile threads of his imagination.

As he began to read, concepts flowed through him like a gentle stream—adventures that spanned worlds, providing glimpses into lives that were both mundane and extraordinary. The characters danced through his imagination, wrapped in rich tales of hope, bravery, and connection. Each narrative threaded the importance of kindness and empathy, sowing the seeds of understanding even deeper into his heart.

The cockroach, now perched beside him, became a silent companion, embodying the spontaneity that swept through Adam's being as he opened himself to the wisdom the nook had to offer.

He discovered stories infused with wonder, wandering characters seeking purpose in their journeys. Each tale fell into place like pieces of a puzzle connecting over a lifetime. Some fables urged him to cherish the simple beauties found in everyday life, while others reminded him that even in trials, there was an opportunity for growth and learning. Adam was captivated, feeling a growing sense of intimacy with not only the books but also the essence of the world that existed both within the pages and in his own tender heart.

It became apparent: the glimmering cockroach was more than just a whimsical guide leading him through this enchanted space—it was a symbol of the spontaneity and freedom waiting just beyond the surface of his everyday life.

He began to reflect on the times he had let fear hold him back—moments that stifled the bubbling excitement within him, keeping him tethered to the mundane. As he flipped through the pages, he cherished the notion that every flick of the cockroach out of the periphery was an invitation to embrace the unfamiliar, to invite whimsy into his life and actively participate in the tales unfolding before him.

The freedom offered by the stories filled the hidden corners of the library, and he felt himself gradually liberated by their potential—the chance to become part of every adventure he read. In this sacred space where time stood still, the boundaries disappeared, allowing him to imagine himself not merely as a passive observer but as an active participant in the narrative.

With each page he turned, he could feel the shift within himself; the palpable spark of joy and inspiration shone through the humid air, intertwining with the dust that surrounded him. The cockroach, still shimmering, moved closer, as if nudging him toward the next lesson, his tiny presence a reminder to embrace the unknown.

Adam's fingers danced over the next dust-covered tome, eager to uncover more. The library began to feel alive around him, thumping with excitement as if it conspired to breathe adventure into his spirit. Each word, each story unveiled another layer of enchantment, beckoning him towards further explorations.

He lost track of time, absorbed in the magic of what lay before him. He lost himself in this old, forgotten nook—the mysteries of what lay behind each cover feeding his childlike wonder. The cockroach scuttled back and forth—like a playful spirit nudging Adam to leap into one story after another, to affirm his right to explore and forge connections with the many tales dancing in his mind.

In this moment, Adam was not merely a boy lost in a library. He was a storyteller, a hero, a creator, living within the threads of the narratives surrounding him. He sought out the shimmering lessons hidden amongst the stacks, etching each experience deeper into the fabric of his being. Each discovery pulled him along with laughter, warmth, and an insatiable curiosity—the spirit of the cockroach guiding him further into the wonder of existence.

As the pages turned and dusk settled outside the window, he gazed at the cockroach—a being so fragile, yet so resilient, embodying spontaneity and the joy of exploration. Adam made a promise to himself in that dimly lit nook: he would not shy away from moments that asked him to leap, to create, to dance across unknown landscapes.

With newfound courage swelling in his heart, he felt a gentle shift around him, a subtle yet profound reminder that stories are not simply written upon pages; they are the essence of life itself, an unfolding journey—the laughter, the heartaches, the connections that bind us, interpreting existence through shared experiences.

And as Adam closed the book in front of him, the cockroach glimmered one last time, sealing the bond they had forged within this sacred space. The weight of the lessons shared lingered in the air, and he knew that with each flicker of silver, there remained a world waiting to be explored, ready to invite whimsy into every corner of his life.

A Father's Shadow

Bobby's Morning Routine

Bobby's morning began with the sound of the alarm clock slicing through the fog of his dreams, a harsh awakening to the responsibilities that awaited him. He reached out, groggy and slightly disoriented, to silence the relentless beeping. The familiar surroundings of his bedroom came into focus: scattered art supplies, unopened sketchbooks, and a half-finished canvas leaning against the wall, all reminders of the creativity that once flourished here.

With a deep sigh, Bobby swung his legs over the side of the bed, his feet finding comfort on the cool wooden floor. He sat there for a moment, letting the stillness of the morning embrace him. Outside, the first rays of sunlight broke through the curtains, casting soft shadows that danced across the room. It was a beautiful sight, one that usually sparked inspiration, yet today it felt like another reminder of the dreams deferred.

He moved to the bathroom, mechanically brushing his teeth and splashing cool water on his face. As he glanced in the mirror, his reflection seemed like a stranger; the bags under his eyes and the hint of stubble suggested sleepless nights filled with worry. He was a father, sure, but he was also a painter—a title that felt almost alien now. The canvases, vibrant with color in his memories, lay untouched and abandoned, suffocated under layers of dust and neglect.

Breakfast was next on the agenda. Bobby found himself wandering into the kitchen, his hands operating on autopilot as he set the kettle to boil and pulled out a bowl for cereal.

Amidst these repetitive motions, his mind drifted to Adam, his curious son, who now had a tendency to explore life with wonder instead of cautious trepidation. Adam awoke each morning filled with the enthusiasm of a kid on Christmas morning, and Bobby was determined to nurture that spark. But the pressure of adult responsibilities tugged at him, whispering doubts about his capabilities as a father and an artist.

The kettle whistled, its shrill cry signaling that water was ready. He poured it over tea leaves, inhaling the comforting aroma that wafted upwards, creating a moment of calm amidst the chaos in his thoughts. This was a routine meant to ground him, yet he often felt like he was merely passing through each day without truly engaging.

Once breakfast was ready, he savored a few bites while scanning his phone for messages. The screen lit up with notifications, mostly work-related: emails from clients demanding updates, reminders for deadlines creeping up, and inquiries about the projects he had yet to dive into. Bobby tried to push them aside, rolling his shoulders back in an attempt to release the tension, but the pressures came rushing back. Time was slipping away, and he felt increasingly overwhelmed.

Then came the sound of little feet padding down the hallway. "Dad!" Adam called, his voice bright and unfiltered by the weight of responsibility that had settled on Bobby's shoulders. He could hear the excitement bubbling in his son's tone, a delightful contrast to his own weariness. Adam burst into the kitchen, his hair a tousled mess and his eyes sparkling with the adventures that awaited them. The sight of his son shed light on Bobby's gloom, if only momentarily.

"Good morning, buddy!" Bobby replied, a smile spreading across his face despite the heaviness in his chest.

"What are we doing today?" Adam asked, bouncing on his feet, clearly in the mood for a grand adventure.

Bobby opened his mouth to respond, to promise his son an exciting day, but paused. He found himself lost in thought, racking his brain for something meaningful, something that would inspire Adam—the kind of experiences he wished he'd had as a child, the kind that fueled his artistic fire. But as his responsibilities loomed larger, it felt like the spontaneity of those dreams was fast evaporating, like mist under the sun.

"Um, I was thinking we could go to the library later, maybe explore some new books," he said, the words feeling inadequate in comparison to Adam's bubbling enthusiasm.

"Can we see the magical books with the shining pages?" Adam exclaimed, his imagination ignited.

"Sure, kiddo. We can find those," Bobby replied earnestly, hoping to muster his own excitement alongside his son's fervor.

The possibility of the library resonated deep within him— a place filled with boundless stories, knowledge, and whimsy that could paint the dullness of reality with splashes of color. Hadn't he once dreamed of creating stories and art that could ignite emotions just like that? He felt the tug of something buried within, a whisper from the depths of his creative soul that he longed to awaken.

As they finished breakfast, Bobby caught glimpses of Adam, always vibrating with energy, the way his son asked questions about everything—life, the world, their uncharted adventures. Bobby remembered a time when that same energy pulsed through him, during late-night painting sessions filled with reckless abandon as colors flowed seamlessly onto the blank canvas.

"Dad, can you draw for me? Can we make a story together?" Adam asked, his eyes wide, pleading for the kind of connection a child craves and, in many ways, a connection Bobby craved too.

"Of course," he replied, although a part of him felt heavy with the knowledge that finding the time to draw or create was just another dream lost among the daily necessities of life. "Let's finish breakfast first!"

The transition into their morning routine felt normal enough, yet weighed with complexities—cleaning up the breakfast dishes, dressing Adam for the day, and then the usual struggle to find matching shoes. All the while, Bobby's mind swam with thoughts of unfinished canvases and longing for artistic expression. He felt the responsibilities piling up as if they were physical burdens weighing down on him.

After they rushed through their morning rituals, Bobby glanced around the small house they shared, a cozy yet cluttered space filled with remnants of his past artistry and a sense of hope shadowing the present. Each painting he had hung on the walls was a fragment of his dreams, remnants of who he was before parenthood swept him up in its whirlwind.

"Are you ready for school?" Bobby asked gently as Adam settled into his chair, legs swinging in anticipation.

"Yeah! Can we read the story you told me about the dragon tonight?"

"Absolutely! We can turn that into a real adventure later," Bobby promised, though a knot formed in his stomach as he realized he might not have the energy to keep such promises—yet, he could not deny that spark of imagination that twinkled in Adam's eyes. It ignited something close to hope in him, and that was enough for Bobby to push forward despite his internal doubts.

As the minutes ticked by and the old clock on the wall ticked in rhythms of time, Bobby finally guided Adam towards the door. They ventured outside, the air refreshing yet tinged with the weight of their reality—a day full of countless chores, responsibilities, and the often-unacknowledged dreams of a struggling artist.

Each day, the commute felt like he was gliding through life without firmly grasping any meaningful moment. But Adam seemed to embody the spirit of spontaneity that Bobby had lost, and through him, Bobby found glimpses of the happiness running deeper than the daily grind.

After dropping Adam off at school, Bobby drove back home, his surroundings now tinted with muted tones of gray. He pulled into the driveway, shutting off the engine while contemplating the blank canvases waiting for him inside. Life had settled into an unrelenting routine, a cycle that gripped him firmly, and he couldn't help but wonder how he had reached this point, where creativity felt like a distant memory instead of an active journey.

The watercolor palette resting on his easel called to him, but he hesitated, wondering if he could dive back in after so many years spent in the shadows. A quiet struggle churned within his mind, facing down both doubts and desires, each battling for dominance. Bobby grabbed his sketchbook and, without another thought, retreated to his creative corner in the living room, attributing a minute to dreams abandoned in the haze of reality.

Picking up his pencil felt natural, yet foreign, like stepping back into a warm bath only to feel the water turned cold. But with each stroke, memories flooded back—the exhilaration of the first stroke on canvas, the emotions pouring onto the page with every line.

Yet, he couldn't shake the sense that the weight of his obligations anchored him to ground zero, reminding him of the many sessions lost to time. The thought loomed, creating a barrier that felt painfully insurmountable.

He sat there, surrounded by hues of color, shadows of old brushes cluttered around him. The art supplies silently begged him, coaxing forth the wild, unrefined inspiration he used to cherish, yet each day was a battle to prioritize his art alongside the responsibilities of fatherhood. On those days, the brush felt heavy, the ideas trudging through thick fog, stifled under the burden of duty associated with being an adult.

Bobby sighed deeply, releasing a breath he didn't know he was holding. The thoughts circled his mind like vultures, hungry for an opportunity, for a creative spark that could light up the canvas before him. It was a familiar feeling—caught between the desire to create and the necessity to provide, suffocated by obligations while fretting over past aspirations.

Finally closing the sketchbook, he resisted the urge to plunge into his thoughts, recognizing he would only drown in the oceans of 'what ifs' and 'maybes'. There was a constant dance between ambition and responsibility as he reluctantly set down the pencil once again. He couldn't shake the sense of loss inherent in this struggle, the lingering feeling that he had sacrificed part of himself in a world where adult responsibilities seemed to reign.

Bobby hesitated but knew he needed to keep going. He couldn't allow himself to be swept away into the confines of this reality—fatherhood and artistry were not mutually exclusive. Yet each morning, those dreams weighed heavily, a reminder that while he nurtured Adam's creativity, he was often neglecting his own.

Taking a fortifying breath, Bobby rose from the easel. He fought gently against the doubts that gripped him while recognizing that perhaps this routine, mediocre though it felt, was paving the way for the greater path ahead.

As he returned to the kitchen to tackle the dishes, he wondered if there was a way to bring both worlds together, to embrace not just his son's imaginative spirit but also his own long-lost ambitions. Perhaps in teaching Adam about kindness, he could rediscover the very kindness he needed to show himself—a chance to embrace the artist lurking in the shadows amid the crumbling dreams.

Today would not be a day for painting, but it could be a day for possibility. And for every brushstroke left unapplied to the canvas, there were stories waiting, drifting in the air, gently nudging him towards a different way of seeing everyday life—a reminder that art lives in every moment, and parenting could indeed be a canvas just waiting to be painted on.

In the spirit of nurturing creativity, Bobby decided not to discard the dreams that had once seemed so alive and radiant. Every interaction with Adam was a new opportunity to spark inspiration, whether through shared reading, creative storytelling, or drawing pictures together. He believed that by illuminating that relationship, he might just light the path toward his own artistic revival. And thus, the day unfolded, each ordinary moment entwined with the extraordinary—the ordinary magic of fatherhood, setting the stage for a creative renaissance bubbling just beneath the surface.

Reflections of the Past

In the quiet of his workspace, surrounded by scattered tubes of paint and brushes left abandoned, Bobby found himself afloat in a sea of memories. The sunlight filtered through the window, casting golden rays onto the wooden floor, illuminating dust motes that danced like the fleeting thoughts in his mind. He sat on a stool, the familiar scent of linseed oil and turpentine mingling with the fresh aroma of coffee brewing in the kitchen. It was a blend he loved—yet, today, it brought with it a profound sense of longing.

Bobby's hands hung loosely at his sides, fingers twitching slightly as he fought against the weight of a brush that felt foreign against his grip. He gazed absently at a blank canvas, waiting expectantly, much like his own dreams waiting patiently for him to indulge in them. Days like this blurred together, with moments of inspiration often masked by the pressing demands of fatherhood and work.

He leaned back, closing his eyes and allowing the memories to wash over him. Flashes of carefree afternoons spent painting in the sun danced in his mind. He remembered the exhilaration that coursed through him while he experimented with colors, the way the hues danced across his canvases, expressing emotions he sometimes couldn't articulate. He could almost hear the laughter of friends around him, the chirping of birds in the trees—a symphony of unrestrained creativity.

Yet, now, those days felt as distant as the summer skies he once longed to paint. Instead of carefree creativity, the suffocating weight of expectations loomed over him—expectations of being a responsible father and a reliable provider. Each responsibility felt like a thick chain, binding him further from his true self, the artist who once reveled in spontaneous adventures.

As he opened his eyes, gazing back at the blank canvas, the feelings of fear and inadequacy bubbled to the surface.

What had happened to the ambition he once felt?

Bobby was no stranger to fear; it had been a companion for as long as he could remember. The fear of failure was overwhelming, telling him daily that he was inadequate and that he wouldn't be able to support Adam's dreams while chasing his own. Having grown up in a household where artistic aspirations were viewed as frivolous, he felt the echoes of his childhood whisper around him, reminding him of the necessity to conform.

"A painter can't provide," his father's voice echoed in his mind, a reminder of the sacrifices that came with choosing an artistic path. With each reassessment of his choices, bitterness crept in, as did regret, for he had long believed that he had abandoned his artistic voice for the sake of practicality.

Adam was different, bursting with an imagination that Bobby could only admire. He watched his son marvel at the world, exploring it with wide-eyed wonder and limitless creativity. Each brushstroke of Adam's budding talent rekindled a flicker of hope within Bobby, and as he contemplated their stories together, he worried.

Would he be able to nurture that creativity? To guide Adam without stifling him? Bobby's heart tightened at the thought that he might inadvertently push his son toward the very fears that had chased him throughout his own life.

Taking a deep breath, he turned away from the canvas, seeking solace in the faint sounds of Adam playing in the other room. The cheerful sounds of imaginary battles or heartfelt conversations with invisible friends filtered through the door, pulling Bobby out of his dark reflections. Experiencing that unfiltered joy filled him with a warmth that pushed against the chill creeping in from his earlier doubts.

He stepped away from his easel, his feet carrying him toward the sounds of laughter. It wasn't just Adam's laughter; it was the exuberance of youth, an open heart that had yet to experience disappointment or the burden of expectations. Bobby recalled his own childhood dreams, picturing the vibrant colors he wanted to paint and the worlds he wished to create.

"Maybe I can mirror that freedom," he mused silently, realizing that each laugh from Adam was also a call to action—to reclaim his own artistic spirit and encourage his son to explore without reservations.

He wandered to the small storage area where Adam kept his art supplies, a treasure trove of colorful chaos that was a vivid testament to the kid's imagination. There, Bobby found a mixture of crayons, markers, and half-finished sketches taped haphazardly to the walls. Each piece of art told a story, each a window into Adam's soul.

As he rifled through the collection, he pulled out one of the sketches adorned with bold strokes of crayon. It was a whimsical creation—a dragon battling a knight amidst a swirl of stars and planets. Bobby chuckled softly. "This one is magnificent!" He knew that Adam had been spinning tales of courage and magic, filled with all sorts of lessons.

Looking at his son's artwork, Bobby's heart filled with a profound sense of pride. This drawing embodied the limitless potential of creativity, turning mundane afternoons into epic sagas. Adam had a gift for storytelling, and through these drawings, he was constructing narratives of bravery, heroism, and friendship. Each dash of color on the page reflected the wonder he felt while surfing through dreams and imagination—a freedom that Bobby once enjoyed.

In that moment, Bobby understood the pivotal role he could play—not only as a father but as a creative equal, guiding Adam while also rediscovering himself along the way. He could share the joy of creating, allowing their world to become one of shared adventures, where both father and son painted their dreams together.

He returned to his workspace, pulling out a fresh canvas and setting it before him. He felt invigorated, almost electric with newfound purpose. Takashi and Sora, imaginary characters from one of his favorite childhood tales, danced at the edges of his imagination, reminding him of the magic that awaited him if only he'd start anew.

As he mixed colors on his palette, the vibrant reds and blues began to speak to him, murmuring tales of adventure and exploration. Suddenly, the familiar warmth of inspiration wrapped around him, igniting the passion that had lain dormant for too long.

He started painting, letting each stroke echo like a heartbeat—a testament to the joys of life as he embraced uncertainty. He painted not just for himself or his career but also for Adam. The canvas transformed from a blank space into a vivid tapestry of interconnected stories, alive and pulsing with creativity that whispered power and possibility.

And with every layer of paint, Bobby felt boundaries fade away. His own fears wore thin, struggling against the new resolve blossoming within him.

Now there were two dreamers, two adventurous souls navigating the waters of imagination. In painting alongside Adam, he thought, maybe he'd forge a path not just for himself but also inspire a new generation of creativity.

As dusk approached, shadows crept into his workspace. Bobby stepped back, surveying the canvas; a swirling galaxy stood before him, brimming with promise. Each star was a hope, each color a dream unpressed. Perhaps he began to see the correlation between his journey and Adam's—each had the potential to inspire and uplift the other.

Bobby smiled knowingly to himself, resolved to nurture this spark he had rediscovered.

In the twilight, he felt the embers of hope rekindle, igniting aspirations that had slept in him for years. He recognized the need to reestablish connections between realistic expectations and whimsical dreams. One would not diminish the other; instead, they would grow together.

His thoughts swept back to Adam, and the bubbling energy that had driven his child to explore this library world; it had opened a new chapter for them both. He found a deep yearning to harness this opportunity, to share the magic of creativity and exploration with Adam, to dive into uncharted waters together, unraveling mysteries beyond the pages of the story.

Returning to the present, Bobby could almost hear Adam conjuring fantastical tales, playing hero to imaginary villains under the glow of a creative spark. Every exploration Adam embarked on was a reminder to Bobby of adventures yet to unfurl in his own mind. As father and son embarked on this journey together, he felt the weight of the past lighten. Together, they would paint their shared history in hues vivid and bright, propelling each other toward a future inspired by dreams and painted in love.

As Bobby continued painting into the evening, the shadows retreated further from the light, illuminating him in a newfound resolve. The fears that had once chained him began to evaporate into the air, replaced by the vibrant colors that transformed into symbols of hope. He glanced towards the door, knowing Adam would soon come charging in, bubbling with stories of his latest exploits.

With every stroke of his brush, he also forged stories that could be woven, exploring realms in tandem with his son. The reflections of the past had guided him, but no longer shackled him; they became a springboard for growth, an engagement between generations, inspiring two dreamers to glide forth, hand in hand, toward an ever-expanding horizon.

As the last light of the day faded, Bobby took a moment to embrace the silence, the possibilities stretching infinitely ahead of them. In nurturing Adam's dreams, he unearthed the artistic depths within himself; they would marinate together in the vibrant canvas of life.

His journey as a father is now intertwined beautifully with his evolution as an artist—a feat he believed would set the stage for Adams' growth as well; an adventure painted with spontaneity, warmth, and joyous connection.

A Connection Reclaimed

The first rays of dawn crept cautiously through the curtains, casting a delicate golden hue across the kitchen. Bobby stood at the counter, the familiar clatter of pans and dishes echoing in the small space. He poured milk into a bowl, his hands moving almost mechanically as he watched the cereal float lazily to the surface. Thoughts of artwork yet to be completed swirled in his mind, tethering him to an ambition that seemed to drift further away with each passing day.

Despite the routine, there was something different today—an unshakable realization coursing through him. His son would not wait patiently forever.

The familiar sound of footsteps broke through his reverie, and the plump, worn soles of Adam's slippers padded into the kitchen. Bobby turned to meet the sight of his son, hair tousled and wild, his face still streaked with traces of slumber.

But it was his eyes—those bright, curious eyes—that truly captured Bobby's attention. They shone with an untold wealth of stories, an eagerness unfettered by the harsh realities that dulled adulthood.

"Good morning, Dad!" Adam chirped, climbing onto the stool at the counter, swinging his legs with an energy that was both infectious and humbling.

"Morning, buddy," Bobby replied, forcing a smile while suppressing a sigh of the weight he felt pressing upon his chest. It was a daily struggle to navigate the complexities of parenting while yearning to find his own artistic voice, a balancing act he had yet to master.

Adam reached for the cereal, eyes lighting up as he navigated the terrain of breakfast options. "Can I have the chocolate ones today?" he asked, hope woven into his request, brightening the room around him as if each word were a sunbeam breaking through a thick fog.

Bobby hesitated. He appreciated the joy of a simple breakfast, yet he found himself weighed down by the unspoken judgment against indulgence. "Maybe just a little, okay? We can't have chocolate for every meal," he said, attempting to infuse a lesson in moderation within the indulgence.

"Okay!" Adam beamed, clearly happy with the compromise, and he dove into the bowl with abandon. As Bobby poured the cereal into Adam's bowl, watching the way his son savored each bite with pure delight, he felt an unfamiliar warmth spreading in his chest—a stirring of the affection that had always been there, but often overshadowed by his worries.

"How are you doing today?" Bobby asked the question, slipping out more softly than he intended, almost like a prayer echoing across the chasm that had separated them for so long.

Adam paused, looking up from his bowl with wide, innocent eyes. "I'm good! I was thinking about going to the library after school! Maybe I can find a book with dragons!" His eyes sparkled with visions of distant lands and fierce creatures. Bobby chuckled, imagining the adventures that awaited Adam amid the aged pages of forgotten tomes.

"Dragons, huh? That sounds exciting," Bobby replied, forcing a wave of enthusiasm into his voice despite the gnawing thoughts tugging at the edges of his mind. "Maybe I can take you this weekend? We can look for stories together."

"Really?" Adam's eyes grew even wider, bursting with life as though someone had flipped a switch and flooded the room with brightness. "That would be awesome!"

For a moment, Bobby felt invigorated, like a painter stepping back from a canvas to admire the work of art that had slowly come to life. Yet beneath the surface, the unspoken words hung in the air, heavy with nostalgia and the layers of their history. Bobby often felt as though he were on the edge of discovery, peering into the vibrant spectacle of Adam's world while fighting valiantly against the self-imposed chains of adulthood that concealed the very essence of creativity that he had once cherished.

As Adam emptied the bowl of cereal, his enthusiasm flowed far beyond breakfast. "Can we read together after school, too, Dad? You can help me find more books!"

Multiple thoughts fluttered within Bobby's mind, a cacophony clamoring for attention: work projects unfinished, a canvas that longed for the brush's caress, the pangs of guilt for not spending enough time with his son. Yet, he wanted to commit to engaging deeper—wanted to push through the barriers of fatigue and frustrations. He thought of the fading dreams he carried, locked up alongside his aspirations like a forgotten treasure chest buried beneath the sands of time.

"I'd love to do that, Adam. We can make it our adventure," Bobby said finally, the words feeling like a balm upon his weary heart. Adam's face gleamed with excitement, his small fists pumping the air in triumph as he devoured the last remnants of cereal.

The echo of joy bubbled between them, quality time spilling out as they prepared for the day ahead. Bobby watched as Adam slid off his stool, a whirlwind of energy, yet there was a newfound glimmer in Bobby's eyes—a far more sincere enthusiasm that sprang to life, fed by the connection that felt neglected for too long.

As they cleaned up together, Bobby found himself pondering the "how" of his commitment. How could he reclaim the connection that had begun to wane in the wake of adult responsibilities? With every chore they tackled, he felt urged to reflect on their journey, to carve out space for both fatherhood and the resurgent dream of creating art, recognizing them as two sides of the same coin.

"Hey Adam," he began, cautiously broaching the subject. "What kinds of stories do you want to find in the library?"

"Adventure ones! The ones where the kids find treasure and battle monsters," Adam exclaimed, readying himself for the imaginative depths he craved to explore.

"Treasure and monsters, huh?" Bobby smiled, turning to face his son. "What if we added a hero who helps people, too? Someone who shows kindness? Like a treasure hunt that includes helping others along the way?"

"Like a superhero!" Adam exclaimed, eyes twinkling as he connected with the idea. "I could be a hero too!"

"That's right! You can be a hero!" Bobby encouraged, feeling energized by Adam's enthusiasm. He felt a weight lift slightly as they engaged in this lighthearted exchange. It wasn't about simply building a narrative together—it was about intertwining their lives, reconstructing their bond through creativity and shared imagination. Bobby realized then that he too longed to embrace the idea of being a hero, not just for others, but for himself, dispelling the shadows of doubt that had haunted him for too long.

Finished with breakfast, they transitioned to preparing for their respective days. Bobby's thoughts drifted between the responsibilities awaiting him at the gallery and the prospect of rediscovering the imaginative currents that ran deep within their conversations. As Adam dashed off to grab his backpack, Bobby's heart swelled with a sense of urgency. He could feel the ticking clock of fatherhood resonating through the walls of their home, and he could no longer afford to be merely a spectator in Adam's life, letting the waves of creativity crash over him without responding in kind.

"Hey, Adam!" Bobby called out, capturing his son's attention as he descended back down the hallway, a bright backpack slung over one shoulder. "Is there something you've always wanted to create?"

Adam paused, eyebrows scrunching in concentration. "I want to make a story with dragons and treasure! But also about being nice, like finding lost pets!"

"Those sound like incredible stories!" Bobby praised, realizing how much happiness could be sculpted from such innocent fantasies. They held castles, adventures, and the possibility for kindness that both he and Adam seemed to long for.

The door burst open, and they both stepped into the world outside, the cosmic ballet of life awaiting them. Adam hopped down the front steps, dancing playfully on the sidewalk while Bobby walked beside him, feeling a humorous contrast between Adam's exuberance and his own contemplative demeanor.

"Do you ever think about your favorite stories?" Adam whimpered, and Bobby could see his imagination engaged once more. "Like, do they ever feel real?"

"They do, sometimes," Bobby replied earnestly, guided by memories of the stories that had not only shaped him, but those cherished tales he wanted to pass on to his son. "Stories can be really powerful, just like art. They can tell us about ourselves even when we don't realize it."

"Do you ever write your own?" Adam pressed on, his curiosity unwavering.

"I did once, but it seems I haven't for a while. But maybe...I could start again."

"You should! Then we can share stories like we shared breakfast!" Adam exclaimed, skipping ahead, his voice cutting through the morning air like a giddy tune. Bobby couldn't help but chuckle softly, a smile creeping across his face.

They walked the rest of the way to school, adorned by budding conversations that flared with imagination and hope. The moments shifted slowly, like a soft transition from dusk to dawn, as Bobby and Adam reclaimed bits of connection lost in time. With every step, Bobby silently vowed to carve out more moments like these, blending the role of father with the passionate echoes of the artist within, rekindling not just his son's imagination but his own.

After dropping Adam off at school, Bobby felt a wave of determination wash over him. He knew the day ahead still loomed with challenges, art pieces left unsold, uncertainty looming like shadows over a canvas yet to be painted. Yet, he clung fervently to the conversations that he and Adam shared, knowing that even in the smallest interactions, profound connections blossomed and rekindled hope.

With his heart a little lighter, he returned to the gallery, his mind spinning with stories awaiting to be woven. The stark fluorescent lights of the showroom flickered to life, revealing pieces yearning for attention—colors alive with potential, shapes making silent pleas for interpretation. Each canvas whispered its own narrative, mirroring his own life's journey and the tumult of fatherhood.

In those quiet moments with brushes flitting through pigment, Bobby grasped the irony of his dual role as a painter and a father: being a creator wasn't different from being a nurturer, and both could coexist in harmony. If only he would allow the colors of his love for Adam to intertwine with the hues of his creative aspirations.

As he eyed one of the unfinished canvases, a flood of ideas washed over him. An adventure awakened within him, tales of fathers and sons battling their own monsters, exploring the treasures of connection obscured by the chaos of life. He envisioned the story's arc vividly; it spun from the mythic depth of kindness to standing triumphantly against everyday struggles.

With time, Bobby found himself lost in his artistry, letting his brush dance along the textures of fabric and wood. Each stroke held the memory of that morning—of reengagement, of promises to explore the stories that connected them more than he had ever realized. In those moments, he began to reclaim not just his partnership with Adam but also the power of creation itself.

That evening, he carved out space in his workspace for Adam to join him. Before the sun dipped below the horizon, he excitedly prepared his paints and sketchbooks, ready to incorporate his son into his world. It was one fleeting moment of time, but it was enough—a shared embrace of creativity birthed anew, illuminating memories waiting to be painted, adventures waiting to come alive.

When Adam stepped through the door with brimming excitement, Bobby felt grateful. As they clumsily plunged their brushes into the world of vibrant colors and whimsical strokes, he saw their bond strengthen with each mark on their canvas. They began sharing not just their ideas but the hopes and dreams that lay at the roots, weaving together life's narrative into the fabric of art and love.

At dusk, Bobby paused to step back and observe the creation that flourished before him, a vivid landscape of family and creativity unfurling across the canvas. For the first time in what felt like forever, he saw the shared magic—the dragons, the kindness, and the treasure of their bond enveloping all that they touched.

As time pushed on, Bobby and Adam discovered their paths were often woven together within the same stories, showing them the profound connections that could be established when they embraced the intersection of their lives. Each day together was an adventure into the depths of art, creativity, and kindness, both flourishing in their journeys while lighting the way for their future.

In reclaiming their connection, they transformed mundane moments into art, crafting family legacies filled with positivity, rich in empathy. Bobby didn't simply become Adam's father; he became his co-creator, his partner in transformation. And together, they'd embark on a magnificent journey, intertwining their lives one brushstroke at a time.

The Silvery Guide

The Chase Begins

Adam crouched low, peering through the myriad of books that loomed around him like ancient sentinels. The silvery cockroach, glistening like a fragment of moonlight itself, darted ahead with an almost deliberate nonchalance, skittering across the dusty floor of the library. Its movement was a mesmerizing dance, quick yet graceful, leading Adam further into the labyrinthine aisles that seemed to hold secrets of their own.

With each soft step he took, the wooden floorboards creaked underfoot, a gentle reminder of the library's age. It was a sound that echoed the whispers of a thousand stories, stories waiting to be told, lingering in the air like the faintest scent of ink and paper. Adam felt a thrill race through him; the chase had begun, and it was an adventure that beckoned him into the unknown.

The cockroach zigzagged through a narrow passage between two towering bookshelves, each shelf bursting with volumes of forgotten knowledge. Adam followed closely, his heart pounding with excitement. These aisles felt small but cozy, a hidden corridor in a vast world. The cockroach paused momentarily, its antennae twitching as if sensing Adam's presence, then continued on its path, effortlessly leading the way.

As he moved deeper into the library, Adam noticed how the atmosphere shifted. The light became softer, filtering through grimy windows that had not seen the light of day for ages. Shadows danced in the corners, and the thrill of uncertainty electrified the air. He felt as if he were entering a realm completely different from the bustling outside world. Here, in this place, time elongated, bending around him as he pursued this curious creature.

Each corner he turned revealed an array of forgotten histories stored within the binding of books long untouched. Adam marveled at the sight of the spines covered in dust, their titles faded yet holding a potential so rich his imagination struggled to comprehend it.

"Where are you leading me?" he whispered, knowing the cockroach wouldn't answer. The absence of a reply only heightened his curiosity. He strode deeper, eager to uncover whatever mysteries awaited him.

The cockroach darted into an alcove, and Adam followed, stepping over a stray pile of books that appeared to have been discarded in a rush. As he did, he stumbled upon a small desk cluttered with parchment and quills, remnants of a past vibrant with creativity. A part of him wondered about the person who had once used this space. Did they share their own tales, writing their thoughts down in the quiet solitude of the library?

The cockroach paused again, almost as if it wanted Adam to take a moment to absorb the surroundings. He glanced around, his wide eyes drinking in the scene. The spines of books here were adorned with intricate designs; some had been gilded, their titles shimmering, detailed letters catching the dim light in a way that made them appear alive. He reached out and brushed his fingers along one book, feeling the cool grooves beneath the surface. In this moment, he understood: forgotten knowledge was not merely dust and pages; it was a living tapestry of stories and wisdom waiting for someone to listen.

Suddenly, the cockroach took off again, prompting Adam to hurry after it. He dashed from the desk, careful not to trip over books that threatened to spill from the shelves. As he moved forward, he couldn't shake the sensation that the library was speaking to him with a thousand quiet voices, each telling its own tale.

The library felt like a maze, each turn revealing more unexpected corridors, dusty corners that had been overlooked by readers long gone. Each section he passed held the promise of adventure; science fiction, world history, ancient myths— they were all waiting patiently for someone who dared to navigate their depths. The cockroach threaded through these sections, teasing Adam with its fleeting presence, as if it knew it was leading him to something beyond mere curiosity.

His footfalls began to echo louder in his ears, a stark contrast to the hush of his surroundings. The cockroach seemed to appreciate the rhythm, occasionally pausing just long enough for Adam to catch his breath before barreling ahead again, a silvery streak against the backdrop of fading wood and leatherbound tomes.

As he ran, the realization began to settle within him—this was not just a random chase; it felt like a pilgrimage, a quest for knowledge nestled in the open hearts of these forgotten pages. Each book contained the potential for adventure, lessons wrapped in tales, waiting for him to unravel.

Finally, they neared a section cloaked in shadows, where the light barely reached. Here, the cockroach paused before a narrow stack of books that seemed to tower like guardians of their sacred knowledge. Adam squinted, inching forward until he could discern the titles. They whispered to him in subtle tones, calling out as if they recognized the spirit of inquisitiveness in his heart.

"Can you hear them?" he murmured, addressing the cockroach seated at his feet. It seemed to sense his question and twitched its antennae expectantly, affirming his thoughts. In that moment, he felt connected to this little creature, both of them seekers on this extraordinary journey.

Pressing deeper into the shadows, he felt the anticipation build; each turn of his head unveiled the mystery of the books that lay ahead. He could see the dust particles dance in the wavering light, each a tiny universe in itself, filled with stories of life lived long before him. The echoes of distant laughter, high stakes, and solemn truths stirred in Adam's mind as he realized that his adventure was not merely a chase but an invitation to explore the rich, intricate history held in these pages.

Suddenly, the cockroach vanished behind a sprawling shelf filled with books bound in deep emerald green. Adam leaned closer, pressing his forehead against the cool wood, squinting into the shadows for any sign of his elusive guide. Then he saw it—the cockroach was now perched on a book that seemed to radiate an invisible allure, beckoning him closer.

He stepped around the corner of the shelf, and there it was: an ancient tome, gleaming with an otherworldly light, catching both the dust and shadows in its embrace. The title was embossed in golden lettering, vibrant despite the wear it had endured through the years. A thin veil of dust covered it, but the book looked alive, pulsing like a heartbeat. The cockroach danced atop it, urging him to take a closer look, its little body twitching with excitement.

"What secrets do you hold?" Adam murmured, brushing aside the dust with gentle fingers.

As he opened the tome, a gust of air rushed from within, lifting the corners of the pages as if the book itself held its breath, eager to share its wisdom. The interior unfolded with a watercolor of golden pages, shimmering under the dim light, reflecting stories that shimmered with potential and life. Adam felt a rush, a thrill coursing through him as if he had found not just a book but a catalyst for adventure.

The cockroach seemed to nod in encouragement, and for a moment, time stood still. The whispers around him became clearer—the narratives intertwined, creating an elaborate fabric of experiences that stretched far beyond the realms of his understanding. This was indeed a library of wonders, and he had only begun to scratch the surface.

Adam flipped through the pages—here were tales of distant lands, characters marked by courage, and stories that stretched across lifetimes. But in the back of his mind, he realized that the most important story was his own, the one waiting to be written in the fullness of his experiences. Volume after volume beckoned to him, but he felt an intimate connection to this one, drawn like a moth to a flame.

The cockroach remained beside him, a loyal companion in this unfolding adventure. Together they had traced the echoes of another world, a world steeped in knowledge only to be found in places like this—a treasure trove waiting to be unearthed.

As the library encased him in its embrace, Adam began to understand the journey was just beginning. The chase wasn't about catching the cockroach; it was about the stories that had already captured him. With renewed resolve, he adopted the spirit of the silvery guide, ready to explore every nook and cranny of this magical repository that had called to him.

"Let's uncover more secrets together," Adam said softly, the jubilant energy igniting his heart as he prepared to delve deeper into the splendors of the library.

Discovering the Unseen

As Adam ventured deeper into the labyrinthine recesses of the library, he felt a sense of exhilaration coursing through him. Each step he took felt like a dance of discovery, a ballet performed with a partner that was unseen but undeniably present— the silvery cockroach, darting between the stacks. The flickering beams of light cutting through the dusty air seemed to illuminate more than mere shelves; they illuminated realms of possibility and imagination that beckoned him with vibrant whispers.

With each turn, Adam was met with rows of books that appeared to shimmer like gemstones in the dim light. The spines, some cracked and others pristine, housed secrets waiting to be unearthed. He instinctively reached out, his fingers grazing the worn leather and textured cloth of the bindings, feeling the pulse of ages gone by. Dust motes danced in the sunlight, glimmering around him like tiny stars, as he began brushing the dust off the spines.

Titles emerged from beneath their layers of neglect, bold and irreverent. "The Enchanted Forest Adventures", "Tales of Forgotten Heroes", and "Mysteries of the Ocean Deep" filled his vision, igniting a flame of curiosity within his heart. Each title was like a siren's call, tugging at the strings of his imagination, drawing him closer to a world where anything was possible. With each discovery, Adam felt the latent passions within him stir awake, each tale promising realms of wisdom and insight that beckoned him to explore further.

He plucked a slender volume from the shelf that seemed to shimmer more than the others. The cover was an ethereal shade of blue, with a delicate illustration of a phoenix rising against a backdrop of stars. It was unmistakably inviting. Adam opened it tentatively, and the pages, some golden and others printed with elegant illustrations, came alive under the gentle caress of his fingers. He read aloud a title that caught his eye: "Wings of Fire: Stories of Perseverance and Triumph." As he skimmed the first few lines, lessons of resilience and courage unfolded before him, each word compelling him to delve deeper into a narrative that resonated with the urges buried within him.

What fascinated him most was how these stories felt like mirrors held up to his own life. He thought of the moments when he had felt the weight of expectations pressing down on him, suffocating his dreams. The characters within the book faced similar struggles, testing their resolve against daunting challenges, daring to defy the odds. Adam's heart quickened, for he realized that he, too, was part of a grand story, one still in the making. The words on the page began to intertwine with his own experiences and beliefs, filling him not just with knowledge but with a reminder that he was never truly alone in his journeys.

In another corner of the aisle, Adam spotted a tattered book with an illustration on the cover—a majestic tree whose branches seemed to cradle the sky. The title read "The Wisdom of the Ages: Ancient Tales for Modern Souls". A sense of familiarity washed over him, as if the book held the answers to questions he had yet to articulate. When he cracked it open, the scent of antiquity wafted around him like an embrace. Each story within promised insight into the human experience, instilling a sense of wonder as he read about wise elders imparting lessons to their curious disciples.

Here, the characters faced trials that were universal—growing pains, moral dilemmas, choices that dictated their very lives. Adam's imagination ignited further as he connected the narratives to his own life experiences, reminding him of his conversations with Bobby and the protruding shadows of their shared moments. Their dialogues, filled with dreams and uncertainties, took on new perspectives as he immersed himself in the text, realizing that the essence of love, sacrifice, and commitment echoed through the ages, binding him to humanity's collective legacy.

As Adam continued to follow the cockroach, the thrill of discovery escalated. He stumbled upon a collection of fairy tales, their pages intertwined with patterns of colorful illustrations. The book's title, "Whispers of Magic: A Collection of Enchanting Stories", made him pause momentarily. Casting aside the mundane task of searching for dusty volumes, he succumbed to the allure of whimsy.

Reading the stories aloud, he conjured visions of brave knights, cunning thieves, and clever princesses who defied the odds. This thread of imagination coursed through him, urging him to explore how acts of kindness could change the course of a tale, and through that lens, he began to reflect upon his own behavior. He recalled an instance when he offered his last cookie to a friend and how simple kindness transformed that moment into a cherished memory. Each tale underscored the ability of small gestures to build connections, like the threads of a vast tapestry.

Inside another nook, hidden behind a series of heavy tomes, he unearthed a book with a shimmering gold binding. It radiated an aura of sophistication, adorned with engravings that seemed to dance before his eyes. The title was utterly beguiling: "Lessons from the Forest: Nature's Gift to Humanity". Adam was instantly captivated.

As he flipped through the pages filled with wisdom inspired by the natural world, he found tales that highlighted the significance of nurturing both the earth and one another. Each story artfully illustrated how nature's cycles mirrored human lives, teaching valuable lessons about patience, growth, and interconnectedness. He envisioned nature itself weaving its narrative, with trees standing tall through storms, their roots interlocked beneath the surface—an effective reminder of the strength forged through connections.

This book also fostered awareness of the bond between him and Bobby, prompting Adam to imagine how they could work together to cultivate their own garden. He envisioned their hands digging in the soil, laughing as they planted seeds, paralleling the joy that came with nurturing their relationship.

Gradually, Adam began to realize that the library was more than just rows of shelves; it was a living organism, pulsing with stories that interconnected across genres, eras, and philosophies. Each title represented a thread that wove together the fabric of human experience. The knowledge contained within these volumes had the potential to breathe life into adventures, igniting a thirst for understanding that could transcend the barriers of time and space.

His excitement mounted as he grasped each freshly discovered treasure, feeling the weight of history in his hands. In doing so, he not only unearthed stories but also unearthed fragments of himself waiting to be acknowledged. Every book was an invitation to ask questions, reflect, and relate, an opening to understand his emotions and the roots of those he loved. This profound realization married his thoughts with the life lessons of generations past, while planting seeds of wisdom in his own heart.

Adam's bond with literature deepened as he absorbed the teachings within, instilling clarity that he was a part of a larger narrative. He imagined the cogs of storytelling turning, interlinked like the wheels on a bicycle, propelling all of humanity forward on the journey of understanding and wisdom.

In the quiet corners of the library, composed of words, ink, and imagination, Adam felt emboldened. He staggered under the weight of the tales—magical and mundane, intricate and simple. The spark transformed into a flickering flame of inspiration that enlarged with every discovery of unseen books, vital portals to the stories that could influence his outlook on life forever.

As he turned the corner once more, the cockroach paused momentarily, as if inviting Adam to consider his next move. He noticed a wooden table, the surface cluttered with relics of thoughts: postcards, bookmarks, notes left behind. Each artifact held the potential for a story, invoking his curiosity to unearth their origins.

One postcard, embossed with an exquisite illustration of a quiet library, caught Adam's eye. He picked it up and began turning it over, discovering it was written by someone who had a profound attachment to books. The words expressed a longing for connection through shared stories, recognizing the magic they often brought into lives.

As he read, Adam's heart swelled with the realization that literature served as a bridge— a portal not just to other worlds but to connect with people across miles and times. Books were threads binding humanity together, a continuous flow of understanding threading through the centuries, guiding individuals through life's trials and triumphs.

Each sturdy volume represented more than mere text; they were lifelines to shared experiences, fables woven by unseen hands echoing the emotions of those who came before him. He felt a surge of gratitude for this space, for the opportunity to be a part of such an enduring lineage of storytelling— one that connected him not only to his own life but to the myriad of lives lived.

With each glance around the library, the silver cockroach a step ahead, Adam could feel the universe whisper its secrets through the pages that called out to him, waiting to be opened. Although the cockroach was a strange guide, it illuminated a pathway both ancient and vibrant, perhaps leading toward uncovering not only the stories of others but tales harbored within himself waiting to rise.

As he deepened his exploration, each book became a brushstroke in a comprehensive portrait of knowledge and imagination. He discovered how tales offered him wisdom and lessons that could shape his character, helping him navigate the complexities of growing up. Every realization fortified a truth within him: that the unseen connections among books, stories, and life itself formed a rich tapestry— one awaiting further, deeper exploration.

Lessons in Every Corner

Adam's heart raced as he followed the shimmering cockroach deeper into the library's confines. The further he journeyed, the less familiar the surroundings became. Dust motes danced in the filtered sunlight, highlighting the labyrinthine aisles that seemed alive with whispers from their parchment residents. Eager to learn what secrets lay hidden amongst the shadows, he let curiosity guide his steps.

As he turned a corner that felt almost forgotten by time, the light shifted, momentarily illuminating a collection of books wedged together on the top shelf. They appeared ancient, their spines cracked and faded. It was as if these tomes held captive stories waiting patiently for someone to come and unlock their potential. He reached up, stretching on his toes, and gingerly pulled one down. The volume landed softly in his palms, a dust cloud erupting into the air as he blew away the remnants of neglect.

With a gentle caress of his fingers over the cover, Adam read the tattered title: "Wisdom Writ in Shadows: Forgotten Stories of the Past." A thrill tingled in his spine as he imagined the tales buried under layers of dust and time. Setting the book aside, he scanned the shelves further, drawn to the age of the manuscripts laden on the lower shelves. Leaning down, he noticed a peculiar, weathered manuscript lying half-open. Its pages trembled slightly as if they were eager to share their secrets if only someone would take the time to listen.

As Adam flipped through the pages, elegant, flowing script greeted him. The ink had bled here and there, creating soft shadows where thoughts might have lingered. Each scrawled letter contained wisdom far beyond any classroom lesson he had ever encountered. Deep within the pages lay a beautiful tale of love lost to the ravages of time, instincts echoing what it meant to forge true connections.

Every tale saturated with emotion ignited a vivid picture in his mind. He could visualize the characters, feel the sharp pangs of their joys and heartbreaks. It occurred to him that these were not merely stories of imaginary worlds but reflections of the journey humanity shared. Adam realized education was not confined to the neat rows of textbooks. These manuscripts held the hand of the past, offering guidance for the unfolding chapters of his own life.

The cockroach danced nimbly past him, beckoning him with its glistening shell, urging him to keep moving. Adam followed, the redolent smell of parchment and ink wrapping around him like a cherished blanket as he ventured deeper into the mystique.

As he continued exploring, the aisles transformed into a cavern ripe for discovery. He came across a small wooden table laden with an assortment of aged papers and preferenced letters. A scrap caught his eye; it was a letter from a child written to their father. The youthful handwriting, filled with careless loops and exclamations, resonated with innocence and love. "Father, I wish to be brave! I want to conquer the world like the heroes in our stories!"

The visceral emotions leaped off the page. Here was a humble epistle that represented a child's yearning to connect with their parent, filled with aspirations gleaned from literature. With every word, Adam felt the pang of longing, but he also felt empowered. The letter was a reminder that dreams are often rooted in the simplest of wants: understanding. The writer had poured out their heart in ink, unyielding in their request for recognition from the pedestal of their father's love.

Using his thumb to smooth the paper, he savored the beauty of that moment, aware that every person who passed through these aisles was also searching for something. Recognizing themselves in the words scattered throughout these pages—be it aspiration, regret, or affirmation—was a shared human experience, a thread that connected them all.

Continuing his exploration, Adam stumbled upon more bodyless notes tucked inside various books, each rediscovery sending sparks of inspiration racing through him. One such note contained a brief observation about kindness, penned in a shaky hand. It read, "Kindness does not come from the heart of one individual but flows from all. Like ripples in a pond, its effects reverberate in ways we cannot see."

He clutched it tightly, rolling it between his fingers as he examined its essence. The implications of such a simple statement were profound. It spoke to him of interdependence, that every act of kindness he offered made a tiny dent in the grand panorama of existence. It expanded his understanding, revealing that life's lessons often resided not solely within the broad strokes of significant events but within the minutiae of daily interactions.

Just then, the cockroach halted before a series of old folios, inching closer as if urging Adam to lean in. Adam approached cautiously, peering at the spines worn by age and neglect. A title caught his eye: "Echoes of Humanity: Collected Traditions and Folklore from Far and Wide." It glowed mischievously, beckoning him to delve into its depths.

He lifted the hardcover, setting it before him on the table, and opened it gingerly. What unfurled was a cascade of tales that stretched beyond borders yet always contained a universal truth about humanity. Stories of generosity borne through narratives of ancient kings, of lost travelers finding solace in the effort of strangers, and of colorful festivals that celebrated the heartbeat of life.

The revelations danced on each page, and his mind embarked on an adventure—not just across time but also through imaginative landscapes. Adam understood that life was woven with the fabric of shared experiences and remarkable encounters created through compassion and interdependence. The cockroach had truly become a guide, revealing to him that every corner of existence brimmed with lessons waiting patiently to be unearthed.

In one of the margins, he noticed a handwritten note that said, "What may seem mundane is but a whisper of extraordinary potential."

How often had he overlooked the beauty nestled in the ebb and flow of his surroundings? Those words rang true, echoing through his thoughts. Every daily encounter offered the promise of revelation; the simple act of exchanging polite words with a stranger or sharing laughter with friends—all were threads woven into the rich tapestry of relationships. They were the stitches that bound people together. As he turned the pages, each story felt no longer trapped between the confines of ink and paper; they breathed and jumped to life.

With each new discovery, Adam embraced the way stories acted as mirrors reflecting pieces of his very own existence. They illustrated his fears and hopes, unlocking avenues to explore—challenges that made up the essence of growing up, beautifully imperfect and multifaceted.

Near the bottom of the folio, he spied a drawing. Someone had taken the initiative to sketch a whimsical tree bursting with vibrancy and life. In its branches hung a multitude of colorful fruits, each labeled with moral lessons: "Compassion," "Perseverance," "Gratitude," and more. This peculiar tree, with all its rich hue, sprang forth from the fertile soil of kindness and empathy.

Feeling the magic of that image, Adam's imagination unfurled like a sail. The visual blend of colors depicted his own vision of what life could be—a garden growing from shared wisdom and nurturing connections. A smile crept upon his lips as he pondered how just these pages held knowledge that could bridge generations.

Inspired, he spread the pages before him and talked aloud to the cockroach, as if sharing his discoveries with an old friend. "Can you believe this? Every corner has a lesson, a nugget of wisdom! Every encounter, every moment we live is ripe with potential for growth and understanding!"

The cockroach paused for a moment, its antennae twitching approvingly, a living affirmation of Adam's unfolding comprehension. Together, they formed a silent pact. One of exploration, pursuit, and discovery—one where each corner served as a world unfolding lightly upon their awareness.

After a while, Adam gathered himself, a growing sense of purpose blossoming within him as he absorbed the atmosphere around him, sensing the delicate interlude of silence shared by the characters that had come before him. It was time to continue on, to embrace the lessons that lay ahead. The cockroach scurried forth, capturing the momentary stillness around them before darting again into a deeper abyss of the library's archives.

With renewed vigor, Adam pressed on, realizing there would always be opportunities to learn threaded within the fabric of existence. Each note, each manuscript was a chance for connection, an affirmation of his burgeoning understanding of the human experience.

As he ventured deeper into the heart of the library, he couldn't help but feel like an explorer in the world of ideas, collecting treasures of insight that would fuel his growth long after he returned home.

And so, with each step into the unknown, Adam embraced the truth that lessons could be found in every corner, not just within the pages of the books, but in the vast landscape of personal experiences waiting to unfold alongside him.

The Golden Book

Finding the Tome

In a darkened corner of the library, where dust motes danced lazily in the shafts of light pouring through high windows, Adam's eyes were drawn to an otherworldly sight. There, partially obscured by the shadows, lay a book unlike any he had ever encountered. Its cover shimmered in hues of gold and bronze, catching the light in such a way that it seemed to pulse with an inner glow, beckoning him closer.

A gasp escaped his lips as he stepped cautiously toward this enigmatic tome. With each step, he felt a magnetic pull, as if the very essence of the book was reaching out to him, calling him to uncover its secrets. The air grew thick with expectation, and even the whispers of the library faded into an awed silence. It was a moment suspended in time, where nothing else mattered; the world beyond the library faded away, leaving only Adam and the golden book.

His fingers brushed against the spine, a flicker of warmth enveloping him like a gentle sigh. The leather was supple, ancient yet vibrantly alive. As he drew the volume closer, Adam could hear a soft, rhythmic humming, resonating from within as if the stories contained were eager to be freed. He felt a rush of energy coursing through him, invigorating his spirit. The allure of this book was palpable; it was not merely a collection of pages and ink but something alive, pulsating with the weight of untold stories and wisdom ripe for the taking.

Adam cradled the Golden Book in his arms, its presence igniting a spark in his imagination. He hesitated for a moment, allowing the tingling anticipation to wash over him, aware that he was on the cusp of something extraordinary. Was this the treasure he had been searching for, the key to understanding a world that felt endlessly complex? He took a deep breath, steadying himself, feeling as if he were standing at the precipice of a great adventure.

With deliberate care, he opened the book. The pages unfolded gracefully, revealing exquisite illustrations that danced across the surface. Each illustration seemed to breathe, bleeding color and life into the library's dim corners. Beautiful landscapes sprawled across the pages—mythical worlds filled with strange creatures, flowering gardens where manners unveiled themselves as enchanting dialogues, and ethereal beings engaged in harmonious exchanges. Each image shimmered with an inviting glow, encouraging him to delve deeper.

As he began to read, the words leaped from the pages like playful whispers carried on the wind. They twisted and turned, inviting him to follow their threads of wisdom. The prose flowed gently, each sentence peeling away layers of uncertainty, enriching his understanding of manners and connections that spanned across cultures and generations. As Adam read, he no longer felt like merely a child in a vast library; he felt like a cherished guest in the company of ancient scholars.

The stories told of kindness and respect, bonds forged through simple gestures—a bow of the head, a warm greeting. They spoke of characters who transcended boundaries, embracing empathy and understanding in ways that illuminated the world around them. Adam's heart raced as he found himself within those pages, imagining the interactions he had observed among his family and friends, noting how they echoed these timeless teachings.

He paused to reflect, recognizing the significance of the lessons unfolding before him. He had often admired his father, Bobby, for his mannerisms, the way he treated people with an inherent warmth. He could see now where those traits stemmed from—the very roots of respect and kindness that transcended generations and fed into the lives we lead. It made him long to cultivate those qualities within himself, to stand proudly and emulate the same spirit of gratitude and love that he had witnessed.

Each turn of the page brought forth new narratives, interwoven with moral lessons. The Golden Book transported him across borders and eras, from the gardens of Kyoto, where the art of tea was taught as a way of life, to the bustling markets of Marrakech, where commerce danced to the rhythm of greetings. He saw himself at the heart of each story, embodying the characters as they navigated the intricacies of human interaction. The echoes of laughter, the sharing of humble meals, and the delicate gestures of respect left imprints on his heart.

In those moments, Adam realized that the essence of what it meant to be human lay not merely in our actions but in our attentiveness to one another. Every gesture bore meaning, and every conversation offered an opportunity to connect on a deeper plane.

As time drifted away, he became conscious of the shifting shadows around him. The library still harbored a palpable energy, the ancient walls ringing with the wisdom of countless souls whose stories had etched themselves into its very fabric. The Golden Book was a magnificent bridge linking the past to the present, each page a stepping stone guiding him toward his own understanding of kindness—an understanding that bridged the generational chasm not just with Bobby but with every individual he would encounter.

With fervor, Adam dug into the depths of the narratives. The richness entwined within the stories had the power to transform, like a painter's brush bringing dimensions to a canvas. He could feel the universe of tales flowing into him, reshaping the contours of his perspectives and illuminating the corners of his mind where doubt had once crept in. The tales held clarity amidst a chaotic world, defining the essential values he desired to uphold and nurture within his own heart.

The longer he stayed engrossed in the Golden Book, the more he felt himself molded by its wisdom. Each story became a candle flickering in the darkness, illuminating paths he had never before considered. He envisioned himself embodying the values he read of—the spirit of kindness, the unwavering commitment to empathy, recognizing their transformative potential.

Finally, as he reached the last story in the tome, a sigh escaped him, a mixture of satisfaction and longing. The narrative concluded with a powerful reminder: that every person is deserving of respect and kindness. The lesson didn't abide by borders or labels; it pulsed with humanity's shared heartbeat, an echo that resonated through time and space.

Adam closed the Golden Book gently, still feeling its warmth radiating toward him. He was no longer just an observer of stories; he had become a participant in the very fabric of these lessons. The realization washed over him like a gentle wave: he held the potential to carry forth these teachings into his own life, to weave them into his interactions with Bobby, with friends, and with the world at large.

As he stepped back from the tome, his thoughts flickered back to Bobby, who had been lost in his struggles of adulthood, seemingly worlds away from the explorations of a child. Adam's heart swelled with the desire to share these newfound insights with him, to bridge the gap that sometimes felt insurmountable. Perhaps the Golden Book could serve as a guide for them both—a catalyst that would illuminate their path toward understanding.

In that moment, nestled among the towering shelves of literature, Adam felt the compelling stirrings of purpose. He would not only be a seeker of knowledge but also a bearer of kindness. Emboldened by the tales of the Golden Book, he resolved to make every effort to connect with his father, to share with him the magic and wisdom he had unearthed. They would navigate their lives together, like co-authors writing their story, informed by lessons that transcended time.

With determination coursing through him, Adam took one last lingering glance at the shimmering cover of the Golden Book before placing it carefully back onto the shelf— its splendor forever engraved in his memory. He stepped away, leaving the shadowy corner of the library behind but carrying the light of its wisdom in his heart. The library was still, the silence pregnant with potential stories waiting to be unraveled, but Adam knew now that he was equipped to traverse that expanse with newfound purpose.

As he navigated back through the aisles, his heart raced with the thirst for connection. He found Bobby inching forward through the library, busy with his own thoughts, his brow furrowed and eyes cast downward—a stark contrast to the high of adventure Adam had just experienced. He approached his father with a bright spark in his gaze, eager to share the treasures he had uncovered.

To him, Bobby was not just a parent who painted in the shadows, but a man with dreams woven into the very fabric of who he was. Adam longed to extend the tendrils of understanding, to bridge the worlds they had both created in their minds. The lessons of the Golden Book had endowed him with a courage he hadn't yet known, and he felt propelled by an urgency to connect, bridge the distance, and bring their hearts to the forefront of their shared realities.

"Dad," he called softly, his voice ringing clear through the hallowed halls of the library. Bobby looked up, surprise flickering across his features, and for a fleeting moment, the burdens of the adult world seemed to lift as their eyes met.

"Let me tell you what I found in this mysterious golden book," Adam said, beaming with a fervor that rekindled hope. The chapter had closed, but a new adventure awaited them both—one that promised to be etched in their lives forever.

The Whisper of Pages

As Adam gingerly opened the worn cover of the Golden Book, a distinct feeling enveloped him—a mixture of anticipation and the solemnity of holding something ancient, something imbued with untold stories. The pages, delicately gilded, beckoned him to delve within, and as he brushed his fingers over the embossed letters, a ripple of energy coursed through him, as if the book were alive.

With his heart racing, Adam turned the first page. Instantly, he was whisked away into a vibrant story. He found himself standing on the edge of an expansive meadow, lush and green, dotted with flowers that swayed gently in a soft breeze. Before him, a majestic castle loomed in the distance, its towers piercing the azure sky.

The story soon introduced a young girl named Hana, whose laughter tumbled like music through the air. She lived in the castle with her wise grandmother, who was renowned throughout the land for her unique gift: the ability to weave stories that held profound lessons about kindness, empathy, and respect. Hana adored her grandmother deeply and often accompanied her during her storytelling sessions, where the townsfolk gathered to listen, their faces illuminated by the glow of lanterns, the air thick with wonder.

As the narrative unfolded, Adam learned that every tale told by the grandmother had a purpose. One evening, Hana asked, "Grandma, why do you tell these stories? What do they mean?" Her grandmother smiled knowingly. "Each story carries the essence of our lives, dear one. They teach us to connect with others, to understand their joys and sorrows, and to embrace the beauty of kindness in every interaction."

Hana listened intently, the seeds of understanding sown in her heart. The next day, while playing by the riverbank, she encountered a stranger—a weary traveler who carried the weight of the world in his eyes. She remembered her grandmother's words and offered the man a simple act of kindness, sharing her lunch and inviting him to rest. The traveler's expression shifted from exhaustion to gratitude, and with each bite of food, he seemed to shed pieces of his burden.

Adam smiled as he witnessed the transformation taking place in the story. He felt an unmistakable connection with Hana, recognizing that small acts of kindness, embodied in her interaction with the traveler, echoed in the truths he learned from his own father. This moment crystallized into an important lesson: the power of compassion transcends physical barriers and can heal even the deepest wounds.

Turning the page, Adam was drawn into a different tale, this one set in a mythical forest shrouded in mist. The protagonist was a spirited fox named Kaito, who seemed to embody mischief. He was known for his clever tricks and laughter, yet beneath the surface, he was restless, easily bored with the day-to-day rituals of life.

One day, Kaito discovered an old, gnarled tree laden with bright red berries. He climbed it in haste, ignoring the cries of warning from his fellow forest creatures about the consequences of overindulgence. As he feasted on the berries, he suddenly felt a shift within the magical grove—the usually welcoming oasis turned hostile, the trees now whispering words of disappointment. Kaito soon realized that his actions carried consequences beyond mere fun; they affected not just him, but all the living things around him.

Adam's gaze shifted as he immersed himself in Kaito's journey. He watched the fox's transformation from a carefree trickster to a responsible member of the forest community. After his regrettable feast, Kaito felt compelled to seek forgiveness from his friends. He realized that true joy comes from shared experiences and respect for the well-being of others, ultimately enriching the lives around him. In this tale, Adam grasped the fundamental lesson of balance—enjoying life without losing sight of the collective harmony.

The next passage pivoted to a legendary land known as Suna'eli, ruled by a benevolent queen who revered the values of respect and dignity. She insisted on treating everyone as equals, despite their backgrounds. During a festival, she encountered an old servant discarded by the royal court, his spirit dulled and his face shadowed by sorrow. With a gentle touch, she beckoned him closer and asked, "What do you wish for the most?" His voice trembled as he replied, "To be recognized. To feel that I matter."

With that simple interaction, a magic course of events began to unfold. The queen, with her heart wide open, took it upon herself to honor the old servant in front of the entire kingdom. She made a point of showcasing his wisdom during the festival, allowing everyone to witness his remarkable tales and respect his contributions. As the crowd listened intently, Adam could almost feel the warmth radiating from their growing admiration. The servant, overwhelmed with joy, beamed with newfound dignity—a powerful reminder that every person holds significance, no matter how invisible they may feel.

As Adam progressed through the pages, he began to notice recurring themes—each story was interwoven with values that transcended age, culture, and time. They offered glimpses into different ways of living that emphasized manners, empathy, and respect. He started realizing that these tales were not just luxuries of fantasy; they were the building blocks of his existence, principles he could actively incorporate into his everyday life.

In a captivating passage, the Golden Book introduced him to a captivating story about a village engaged in a fierce competition every year—a race that determined their leader. The protagonists were two best friends, Li and Kael, who had once shared aspirations and laughter. As the race approached, both friends became consumed by ideas of winning; they lost the bonds that had defined their friendship.

On the day of the race, as they began to run, a sudden storm broke out, causing chaos among competitors. Both Kael and Li, amid the struggle to finish, caught a glimpse of a small child struggling to reach shelter. They confronted a crucial choice: honor their dreams of victory or help someone in need. In a moment that would define their character, the friends chose to sacrifice their aspirations for the safety of the child. The bond of friendship became even stronger; they learned that true success isn't measured by trophies but by the kindness we extend to others.

Adam couldn't help but ponder his own friendships. He recalled instances where competition had overshadowed compassion, transforming a simple connection into a battleground. Through this tale, he recognized that loyalty, support, and camaraderie were far more enriching than fleeting recognition.

Calls of laughter, echoes of old-fashioned etiquette, and lessons in dignity rang through each story like a melodic chorus. With each brush of the pages, Adam absorbed the wisdom interlaced within the fables. The stories danced before him, becoming part of him as he internalized their morals, shaping his understanding of the world.

The tales took on a deeper significance as he found reflections of his family within the characters. His father's struggles to balance work and art mirrored the journey of some of the protagonists, burdened yet striving. Adam recognized the lineage of values being passed down—lessons from his family intertwined with those of the fictional characters, creating a rich tapestry that highlighted their interconnected nature.

Finally, he encountered a story centered on the importance of listening—an ability often overlooked yet immeasurably valuable. It told of a young bard named Elara, talented in the art of music but often too wrapped in her own melodies to hear others. While traveling through a desolate village, she met an old woman who softly requested to tell her own stories of lost music.

Initially dismissive, Elara later realized that the woman's words held importance beyond her understanding. As she listened, the old woman recounted tales of love, loss, and hope, passing down songs long forgotten. In absorbing those stories, Elara transformed her music, creating harmonies filled with layers of emotion that resounded through the village and beyond.

Adam mulled over this lesson. In a world eager for attention, the essence of truly listening unlocked connections and fostered understanding, traits vital in his relationship with Bobby. He understood that compassion often stemmed from genuine curiosity about one another's journeys.

With the sun beginning to set outside the library, casting a golden hue over everything, Adam turned the final page of the Golden Book. A feeling of fullness settled within him; the stories were engraved not only in his mind but in his very spirit. They had become anchors of wisdom guiding him toward a better understanding of himself and others.

As he closed the book softly, Adam reflected on the lessons learned—kindness, humility, respect, and the importance of community. He knew that wielding these principles in his daily life would set the foundation for meaningful interactions, connecting him not just to his father but to the world at large.

Choosing to carry the lessons from the Golden Book forward, he felt his heart swell with a sense of purpose. When he looked up, Adam found Bobby sitting nearby, scribbling in his sketchbook. The bond between them, woven tighter through shared experiences and enriched with lessons from the past, shone brightly illuminated by the lingering magic of stories.

Filled with excitement, Adam approached him, eager to share his newfound wisdom, confident that everything he had read was not merely confined to the characters and plots of legends, but was instead an irreplaceable part of his own journey—one that they would continue to craft together.

Enchantment of Growth

Adam found himself sitting cross-legged on the floor of the library, the faint scent of aged paper enveloping him like a cozy blanket. His hands trembled slightly as he held the Golden Book, its shimmering cover catching the light and reflecting a multitude of colors that danced in the dim corners of the room. Each page felt alive, a gateway not only into stories but into the very essence of life itself. As he turned the first page, anticipation bubbled within him, stirring a deep thirst for knowledge that had always been lurking just beneath the surface.

The words seemed to leap off the page and swirl around him, wrapping him in a blanket of warmth and comfort. Adam's heart raced with excitement; this was more than just a book. It was a treasure trove of wisdom, a magical map guiding him through the winding paths of compassion, empathy, and understanding. The stories within were not mere tales with plots and characters; they were mirrors reflecting ideals he aspired to embody in his own life.

The first story he came upon was about a young boy named Kenji. Kenji lived in a village where kindness was the highest virtue, celebrated in festivals and daily life alike. One day, Kenji discovered an old, weary traveler on the outskirts of his village. The traveler's clothes were tattered, and his face wore the lines of many hardships. Without hesitation, Kenji approached him, offering a warm smile and the sandwich his mother had packed for him.

"Why are you helping me, young one?" the traveler asked, his voice a raspy whisper, laced with gratitude and surprise.

"Because everyone deserves kindness, even if they seem like they don't deserve it," replied Kenji, his bright eyes shining with sincerity.

As Adam read Kenji's words, he felt a sense of recognition. The predicament of grappling with kindness resonated deeply with him. He thought about times when he had been impatient or hesitant to share, particularly with his little brother, Sam. The story of Kenji taught him that true compassion flourishes in places where it is most needed, often directed toward those who seemed unworthy or invisible.

With the flick of his fingers, he turned to the next tale—a daunting story about a brave girl named Mei who sought to understand the world around her. Each day after school, she would visit the elderly woman who lived at the end of her street. The woman had the reputation of being grumpy, known for her sharp tongue and closed shutters, but Mei was drawn to her nonetheless. One afternoon, Mei gathered her courage and knocked on the door. To her surprise, the elderly woman invited her inside.

As they chatted, Mei learned about the woman's life—a tough childhood spent in hardship and loss, forming the walls that made her seem harsh. Through their conversations, Mei discovered that understanding someone's story was the key to empathy and acceptance. The woman spoke with heartfelt candor, recounting her regrets and dreams, revealing the soft vulnerability hidden beneath her tough exterior.

This story struck a chord with Adam. How many times had he rushed to judgment about someone based solely on their first impression? The realization dawned on him that everyone had their own battles to fight, each a unique narrative filled with complexity. Adam imagined himself sitting on that creaky wooden chair in the old woman's living room, listening intently to her stories, discovering treasures buried beneath layers of defenses that others often overlooked. It was a lesson about patience and the importance of making space for others' perspectives.

As he delved deeper into the Golden Book, Adam encountered narratives about forgiveness, generosity, and resilience, each imbued with virtues that felt as if they were embracing him in a warm hug. He found himself connecting with characters in ways that illuminated the profound truths of existence. He envisioned stepping into their world, watching them navigate the choices they faced, and instantly recognizing echoes of his own struggles in their stories.

In a story set in a lush, verdant forest, Adam met Taro, a gentle soul with a heart full of dreams. Taro had a remarkable ability to communicate with animal spirits and believed they possessed wisdom that could transform the world. One day, a ferocious storm swept through the forest, threatening the home of a timid rabbit family. While most animals were preoccupied with their own safety, Taro bravely ventured into the eye of the storm, calling upon the animal spirits he knew to rally together.

"All our lives are intertwined," he proclaimed, standing tall against the howling winds. "If we come together, we can help one another find safety."

Inspired by Taro's bravery, Adam felt an overwhelming desire to be courageous, just as Taro was. The ideals of compassion and collective responsibility resonated within him. For so long, he had operated under a philosophy of individualism, believing he had to face his fears alone. Yet Taro's story was a beautiful reminder that true strength resided in unity, in lifting others as they climbed life's ladders of uncertainty.

Wisdom flowed from the Golden Book like a river, its lessons seamlessly entwining with Adam's burgeoning understanding of the world. He imagined how he could apply these lessons to his life; each story became a stepping stone guiding him closer to the true nature of kindness, respect, and understanding. No longer were these just lofty ideals tucked away in the nooks of his mind—through the enchanted narratives, they felt tangible, accessible.

It was a story of gratitude that struck Adam most profoundly, one that revealed the beauty hidden in simple gestures. In this tale, a poor farmer found joy through acts of giving, whether it was sharing his harvest with those less fortunate or picking flowers to bring a smile to his neighbors. The farmer's grateful heart turned mundane routines into rituals of joy, transforming the village into a haven of love and harmony.

Adam pondered over this concept, wanting to instill gratitude into his own life. So often, he had taken for granted the small blessings—like the warmth of a home, a loving family, and the laughter shared over dinner or getting lost in a storybook on a rainy day. The farmer's life was a gentle reminder that gratitude cultivated happiness, and Adam made a silent promise to himself: he would seek to express more appreciation for the little moments that filled his days.

As the hours slipped away, Adam became deeply immersed in the Golden Book, its pages turning almost magically under his fingers. Each story unfurled like bright petals in a blossoming flower, captivating him with its unique fragrance. He envisioned himself stepping into a realm where wisdom was not just locked away but lived and breathed in a beautiful chorus of narratives.

The clock struck an hour, echoing softly in the library, almost reminding him of the world awaiting him outside. But Adam felt an unshakeable urge to read just one more story. He turned the page once more, and a new tale captured his attention—a powerful narrative about a young girl named

Aiko who dared to dream big in a world that constantly underestimated her.

Aiko lived in a small village famous for its artisans, each mastering a unique craft. Despite her age, Aiko aspired to be a great painter and yearned for her art to express emotions that words could not quite convey. However, the elders doubted her talent, dismissing her aspirations as fanciful dreams. Yet, filled with determination, Aiko painted every day, pouring her heart onto the canvas, defying the voices that aimed to quench her spirit.

"What does it mean to dream if not to do?" she asked the villagers one day, unveiling her art. Her paintings spoke volumes of love, longing, and resilience, awakening the hearts of those who witnessed her creations. In time, her perseverance opened their eyes to the truth that true artistry comes from the rawness of emotion and vulnerability.

As Adam read this tale, his own dreams flickered before his eyes. Often, he felt the weight of people's expectations, like a heavy backpack pulling him down. He realized that Aiko's journey mirrored his struggles to pursue his passions, whether it was painting, writing stories, or exploring the vastness of imagination that lay hidden within him. The lesson he gleaned from Aiko was profound: to chase dreams ardently, to express oneself authentically, and to silence the voices of doubt that threatened to paralyze creativity.

In that moment of clarity, Adam understood that to nurture growth, he had to embrace not only the virtues shared in the Golden Book but also the courage to be vulnerable. The tales he read became a wellspring from which his own growth could flourish.

Each character's journey illuminated the intricate dance between challenges and triumphs, teaching him resilience in moments of despair as he absorbed the essence of their struggles.

With each story that unfolded, Adam felt a profound connection to the past, present, and future—the tapestry of human experience interwoven forever by shared values and unwavering kindness. Soon, a sense of purpose ignited within him; he would carry these lessons with him as torchlights illuminating his path.

Finally, as Adam turned the last pages of the Golden Book, he took a deep breath, feeling elated yet reflective. The stories had not merely occupied his time; they had permanently imprinted themselves upon his heart, echoing with powerful wisdom that transcended lifetimes. He felt invigorated by the knowledge that he was now part of an ongoing narrative—a story that embraced growth in every sense of the word.

He looked up, gazing at the library that had transformed from a mere collection of books into a sacred space filled with echoes of countless lives. The dusty shelves shimmered anew, alive with the whispers of the characters he had connected with so intimately. This enchantment engulfed him as he recognized the transformative power of stories—not just for him but for all who sought their wisdom.

Adam grinned, deciding then and there that he would share this newfound wisdom with his father, Bobby. It was a treasure trove he could gift to others, transcending generations. With each step back through the aisles, he felt a deeper understanding of his responsibility in embodying the lessons he had so joyfully received.

As he began his journey back, the Golden Book's lessons flowed through him like a gentle stream—beautiful, powerful, and infinite—and he knew that the threads of understanding, kindness, and respect woven through the stories had forever changed him.

And thus, the enchantment of growth became a part of his very being, echoing ever more vibrantly within his young heart.

A Lesson in Kindness

Bobby Reads Along

Bobby stood at the entrance of the library's reading nook, a slight frown creasing his forehead as he watched Adam immersed in the pages of the Golden Book. Sunlight filtered through the tall windows, casting elongated shadows that danced across the floor, igniting Adam's surroundings with an ethereal glow. The vibrant illustrations within the book seemed to leap to life, and though it was a world he yearned to join, Bobby felt tethered by an invisible weight.

He had always envisioned himself as an artist, a storyteller in his own right, but the responsibilities of fatherhood and day-to-day tasks often felt like an encroaching fog. As the chair creaked beneath him, he caught the flickers of joy on Adam's face—a joy that seemed to flicker just out of reach for him.

"Dad, come see this!" Adam's voice rang out, laden with excitement as he pointed to the pages aglow with gold, his eyes sparkling with discovery.

Reluctantly, Bobby shuffled closer, unsure of how to bridge the chasm of imagination that seemed to separate them.

"What's it about?" he asked, the words tasting sour in his mouth. He felt disconnected, as if asking a bright child about the intricacies of watercolor painting when he himself had long abandoned the easel.

Adam leaned closer to the book, whispering, "It's a story about a brave mouse who goes on an adventure to find a lost treasure, but along the way, he learns about kindness and friendship." He glanced up, unconsciously searching for his father's encouragement.

For a moment, Bobby saw a flicker of hope in Adam's expression, a glimmer of the bond they shared. Though Bobby often felt like a worn-out guide, wrestling with temptation to retreat back into the shadows, he possessed a flickering desire—not just to capture Adam's attention but to let himself be captured, too. "Can I read it with you?" he asked, startling himself with the sincerity of his request.

Adam's face radiated joy as he eagerly scooted over, creating space for Bobby among the scattered cushions that enveloped them like a soft cocoon. Bobby settled in, the sensation of warmth creeping in as he held the book, its golden pages shimmering invitingly.

As Bobby began to read aloud, the words flowed over him like a gentle stream. The brave mouse, whose name was Hoshi, ventured through forests and meadows, overcoming obstacles while maintaining his courage and compassion. Each page revealed a new obstacle, yet Bobby found himself resonating with the underlying themes. Hoshi faced moments of doubt and fear, grappling with choices between self-preservation and the greater good of his friends. There was an authenticity to Hoshi that Bobby couldn't deny—an echo of the artist yearning to create while performing the daily rituals of fatherhood.

With every turn of the page, Bobby's heart began to swell. Stories and lessons danced around truths he had long forgotten: the strength found in vulnerability, the importance of being present, and how kindness forged unbreakable bonds. He paused mid-sentence, catching Adam's curious gaze, and for the first time in weeks, something unfurled in his chest.

"What do you think Hoshi will do next?" Bobby ventured, his voice softer than he intended.

Without missing a beat, Adam replied, "I think he'll choose to help his friend instead of running away. Because that's what heroes do!"

A smile tugged at Bobby's lips. "And what does that say about Hoshi?"

"Um... it means he's really brave! And kind! Kindness is super important!" Adam's enthusiasm was infectious, and he leaned forward, eyes glimmering with sincerity.

With each subsequent act in the tale, Bobby became more engrossed; the more he read, the more he began reexamining his own life. Hoshi confronted individuals secluded in pain and suffering, offering support where others had deemed it unimportant. Bobby couldn't shake the growing poignancy pushing at his core.

Admittedly, he had neglected moments of tenderness in his relationship with Adam. The demands of his art career loomed large, often eclipsing the simple joys of their connection. The weight of his aspirations mingled with parental obligations, leaving little room to explore the beauty woven into their day-to-day interactions.

As the story unfolded, Hoshi's triumphs and setbacks stirred painful reflections within Bobby. He remembered instances from his past—a missed chance to share an adventure with Adam or a moment where he hastily prioritized work over play. Those instances loomed larger in his mind, each overshadowing what could have been a cherished memory.

He turned a page, revealing Hoshi's moment of doubt. The mouse stood on the precipice of a decision, staring into the uncertainty below. Adam gasped, his finger tracing the illustration where Hoshi's heart was visibly torn. Bobby understood that feeling all too well; the struggle between ambition and affection was often a rigorous climb laden with uncertainty.

"Dad, do you think he will fall?" Adam asked, wide-eyed. Bobby hesitated, taking a moment to reclaim his thoughts.

"Sometimes we must take risks, Adam. Falling can lead to learning something important if we dare to try again."

Adam nodded appreciatively, a semblance of comprehension dawning upon his young visage. Bobby felt buoyed, realizing that they were embarking on a shared experience—an expedition of emotional tumult threaded with narratives of growth. Underneath heartfelt words, Bobby felt his barriers start to crack.

As they progressed further into the adventure, Hoshi encountered creatures who had once been friends but had been misled by jealousy and misunderstanding. The mouse's endeavor to mend bridges reminded Bobby of his own relationship with Adam—how easily disagreements could fracture their connection.

It struck Bobby that, just like Hoshi, he had grown accustomed to operating on autopilot, misreading his son's needs for acceptance and kindness. A warm flush crept up his neck as he contemplated missed opportunities for connection.

"Can we always find a way to be kind?" Adam asked innocently, tilting his head as he shuffled closer.

"It's not always easy, buddy, but yes, kindness is a choice we have to make each day," Bobby replied, feeling the truth of those words resonate deep within.

As the duo neared the climax of the mouse's journey, Hoshi ultimately gathered the courage to act against the tide of expectation. Bobby felt a kinship fuse between his life and the character's narration. It was not simply Hoshi's story alone, but an exploration of absurd tags shackling attachment. Hoshi's choice to stand up for others illuminated how loyalty and courage entwined when fueled by kindness.

Bobby's heart raced as he absorbed the words, realizing that he too had power—the power to exhibit kindness, not just toward Adam, but in every small interaction that propelled their lives forward. Through the encounter with Hoshi, he perceived a poignant lesson: that kindness was, in essence, an extended hand bridging the gaps left by his distractions.

When they reached the conclusion of Hoshi's adventure— a moment defined by a joyful reunion and heartfelt appreciation—Bobby looked at Adam, who was perched at the edge of his cushion, visibly enthralled. "What did Hoshi learn?" Bobby prompted, in hopes that Adam might reflect on more than the surface excitement built through tales.

"Um, he learned that helping others makes him feel really good inside! And it's super great to have friends!" Adam exclaimed, bouncing slightly.

"That's right. It's wonderful to share those moments of kindness," Bobby reflected, the weight of clarity settling over him. "You know, Adam, Hoshi really made a difference. Kindness isn't just about grand gestures; it's about the little moments, too. Every action, no matter how small, can ripple outwards. Don't you think?"

With earnestness in his voice, Adam replied, "Yeah! Like when I share my toys, or when I help you cook!"

A swell of emotion welled within Bobby, gratitude pooling toward the center of his chest. It dawned on him that these small efforts—silly moments of concocting snacks or adjusting an artwork—were fundamental in teaching Adam about connection and empathy. The simplest actions carried greater weight than he fathomed, providing rooms for warmth.

Pushing forward, Bobby intended to embody that lesson, not merely through words but through practice. As he and Adam started to align themselves with moments of shared understanding, he vowed to make space for kindness in his heart. The external pressures that had often felt paralyzing began to shift. With a Dedicated focus, he leaned into the foundation of understanding—an artist's haven opened by love and exploration.

A few moments passed, and Bobby's attention was drawn to the inviting glow of the Golden Book resting between them. He shut it softly, feeling a deep-seated craving to foster a connection that would bloom beyond the library walls.

"Hey, let's talk about the stories for a bit, yeah? Maybe we could come up with our own?" He met Adam's eager gaze, excitement igniting once more.

Adam beamed, his eyes alight with wonder, as he nudged his father. "Like, what if Hoshi had a sister who wanted to go on an adventure too? They could explore different places!"

Bobby's heart raced. "I love that idea! How about they go to a fantastical world where animals talk and teach them new lessons?"

"Yes! And maybe they encounter a wise owl who shares secrets about friendship!" Adam bounced up and down, the thrill of creation sweeping through him.

"What if we write down our ideas and draw pictures afterward?" Bobby suggested. A fire ignited within him as he realized how swiftly he had shifted from a desaturated state of reluctance to a realm bursting with vibrancy.

As the duo delved into their shared fantasy, the thread of understanding fortified by Hoshi's tale weaved its way into their relationship. The day faded gently; the library with its hushed tones became a sanctuary of co-creation, a weaving together of adventure and affection.

In moments like these, Bobby understood that the stories would continue to echo in the fabric of their daily existence. Each word breathed the essence of love and lessons well-spent, a reminder that kindness wasn't just a lesson learned; it was a path forged anew, together. Every laugh shared and each imaginative journey embarked upon was a small step in reclaiming that connection, a binding thread on a tapestry woven through time.

In the warm embrace of their imagination, Bobby saw shades of his former self rediscovering joy. Instead of looking into the depths of what once held him back, he was finally learning to bask in the light of creation and kindness as he fashioned new promises into the future.

For everything seemed to pulse alive around them, the very air thick with the eagerness of untold stories waiting to be uncovered. Bobby allowed himself to fully absorb that moment—an expansive pocket in time where worry faded, dreams flickered, and kindness blossomed in silences shared.

From that day forth, the bond between Bobby and Adam grew. Each page they read together became not just a glimpse into another world, but a vital stepping stone paved in understanding—a gentle reminder of the power woven through the space of storytelling, exploring, and above all, kindness.

Moments of Reflection

Bobby narrowed his eyes and leaned closer to the window, watching the clouds drift lazily across the sky. The pale autumn sun filtered through the leaves, casting dappled patterns on the floor of his small studio. The remnants of breakfast lingered in the air, yet his attention was no longer on the morning; it had shifted to the pages laid open before him—the Golden Book, glistening with secrets and shrouded in mystery. He had begun reading alongside Adam, inhaling the essence of stories imbued with lessons on kindness and the strength that empathy could foster between people.

Yet, as the words wove in and out of focus, Bobby's thoughts ventured to that hallowed chamber of his mind: the past. Past mistakes danced like shadows, each adorned with the luminous glow of missed opportunities, moments he could have seized to be kinder, to connect deeper with his son.

The first flashback struck him like an unexpected gust of wind. He remembered the day Adam was born, a vivid tableau of emotions—excitement, fear, joy, love. Bobby had held his newborn boy for the very first time, feeling as if he could encapsulate the whole world in that single moment of tenderness. He could nearly hear the gentle cooing sounds of the infant, the sweet fragrance of baby powder, the softness of Adam's skin against his own. But it was also the time when Bobby was grappling with his artistic identity, torn between paints and diapers.

He recalled those first few months when he returned from the hospital, overwhelmed by the weight of responsibility. When Adam cried, Bobby often felt the urge to retreat into his art, seeking solace in his unfinished canvases. He had seen it as a necessary escape, convinced that it fueled his creativity. Yet, he failed to realize how this distance affected Adam in ways he couldn't have imagined—how it stifled the precious bond they could have nurtured together.

"Your father loves you, little man," he had murmured in the quiet of those early mornings, barely looking up from his brushes as Adam lay in his crib, eyes wide with wonder, searching for his father's gaze. Bobby's whispers were heartfelt, but the absence of his presence meant more than any words he could convey. As the brushstrokes of his paintings grew bolder, his relationship with his son felt simultaneously muted, distant.

Days turned to months, and he was whisked into an exhaustive rhythm of balancing work and family. He could still hear the echoes of Adam's laughter, yet they were often drowned out by the cacophony of integrated existence: late nights at the studio, hurried lunches, and coffee breaks lost in thought. As a toddler, Adam would often tug at Bobby's pant leg, eyes wide and hopeful, asking him to put down the brush just once, to show him the beauty that lay within the strokes.

Each time, Bobby had brushed those requests aside, eager to perfect his craft, unaware that his son was craving his attention and affection more than he realized.

The next flashback unfolded before him like a scene from a familiar movie: Adam's first day at school. Bobby remembered feeling a mixture of pride and worry as he watched his little boy take tentative steps toward the entrance, backpack bouncing against his small frame, a vibrant chalk drawing clutched tightly in his hand. The teachers welcomed the students with open arms, encouraging smiles and warmth—a stark contrast to the knot tightening in Bobby's stomach.

He had promised that morning to be present, to listen, to ask about Adam's day and engage with the whirlwind of experiences that awaited him. But when Bobby returned home, exhausted from the pressures of life, he found himself losing focus. Instead of asking about his son's adventures, he buried himself in work, looking through invoices for unpaid bills, seeking out inspiration he craved despite it being an unending stream of demands.

It wasn't until a week later, during a fleeting moment at a community event, that he learned of Adam's struggle to make friends. The way Adam's eyes glimmered with hope when he told Bobby about a classmate, only to have the conversation dissipate like a wisp of smoke as Bobby glanced away, was a memory that haunted him. This revelation struck deep, the moment circling back through the pages of the Golden Book, echoing lessons about kindness and connection.

"Be kind, not just to others but to yourself," a passage whispered, leading Bobby closer to the truth about his own heart. It seemed almost cruel how he'd roamed beyond the landscape of Adam's world when all his son truly needed was a father who would participate fully, openly.

The realization that he had missed countless opportunities flooded over him, cascading like the very leaves dancing outside. Each moment that he hesitated to connect, to show interest, reverberated back through his recollection. They were like crescendos in an unfinished symphony—moments that could have sung kindness, laughter, and warmth into their home. Instead, silence often prevailed.

His chest tightened as he remembered other moments, quiet freeze frames marking the loss of connection. Birthdays where he had promised Adam a special day filled with cake and laughter, but work deadlines cast shadows, dimming those bright celebrations until they were mere afterthoughts. Family gatherings that stirred anticipation—a table set with vibrant food and mingled laughter, yet Bobby found himself checking his phone, consumed by adult concerns instead of embracing the pure joy of being present with Adam.

Even the simplest of gestures often fell victim to oblivion. A hug offered on a day filled with grumpiness was replaced with dismissive laughter. The look of confusion on his son's face was etched vividly in Bobby's mind—Adam searching for understanding, longing to feel valued and loved through small moments that he misinterpreted as insignificant.

Now, in the solitude of his studio, with the Golden Book's pages whispering early morning secrets filled with wisdom, every mistake crystallized into amber, revealing lessons on kindness. He was being called forth to reclaim the tender moments he had allowed to slip through his fingers. It struck him that changes could begin right now, in this very moment.

Slowly, a sense of determination seeped into his core. The past could not be rewritten, but the future was wide open, a blank canvas ready to be filled with colors of love and understanding. Bobby acknowledged this transformative power he held within himself, and with that acknowledgment came the birth of an idea—a conviction to start anew.

With newfound resolution, Bobby glanced at Adam as he sat cross-legged on the floor, absorbed in his reading. The boy's eyes sparkled with glee, as if he had unwittingly taken on the role of a guide through this labyrinth of life. This image brewed warmth in Bobby's heart, coaxing forth an array of affirming emotions, giving him the courage to commit himself to nurturing their bond like never before.

He recalled passages from the Golden Book that illustrated simple acts of kindness as bridges to greater understanding—stories of characters who made the effort to listen, who sat with one another and really saw each other through the lens of compassion. Through these tales, Bobby felt the resonance of a shared purpose emerge. The idea that kindness didn't need to be extravagant; it could be offered through simple, genuine gestures that spoke volumes.

Inspired, he envisioned the possibilities: intentional sounds of laughter, crafts made together, lazy afternoons filled with breathless stories, and spontaneous adventures—moments where they would celebrate each other, breathe together, and cherish their time as a family. The beauty of the mundane and the extraordinary intertwined like vines twining together—feeding each other, cultivating a thriving relationship amidst the everyday chaos.

The idea of nurturing their relationship ignited a new flame, breathing warmth into Bobby's heart. He envisioned starting with small acts—setting aside time each evening to ask about Adam's day; to really listen without getting lost in the intricacies of his mind. A commitment to reach for Adam's hand when they watched the sunset together, reinforcing that he was there, not just in body but in spirit.

This clarity transformed Bobby's understanding of kindness from abstract to tangible—a powerful bond forged through commitments to show up every day, to recognize Adam's need for a father willing to share in life's simple joys. The hesitation that had once surrounded his heart was replaced by a sense of purpose that felt almost divine.

As he turned another page in the Golden Book, he couldn't help but smile, feeling buoyed by hope and revitalized aspiration. He realized that this journey through literature had become more than an escape; it was an invitation to grow, to change, to recommit to a role he had almost overlooked in his pursuit of material success. The lesson was simple yet profound: each day presented an opportunity to choose kindness, to nurture love, and to embrace the relationship with his son as a vital element of his artistic expression.

The sun dipped lower outside the window as Bobby placed the Golden Book on the table, feeling invigorated. He rose from his seat, resolved to seek Adam out, to make the leap from his reminiscing to action. Each missed opportunity he had reflected on would no longer be a weight, but a provision of energy that would propel him forward into the embrace of those fleeting moments.

Stepping into the living space, he caught sight of Adam, still poring over the pages of the Golden Book, a look of glee etched across his face. Bobby watched for a moment, feeling the warmth of joy ripple through him. In the soft light of the setting sun, he approached his son with purpose.

"Hey, buddy," he said, a smile spreading across his lips.

Adam's head snapped up, his expression brightening instantaneously. "Dad! Look at this one!" He raised his finger, pointing to a colorful illustration.

Bobby knelt beside him, peering at the page. "What's this about?"

"It's about a dragon and a boy who shared adventures!" Adam exclaimed, his enthusiasm pouring over like a radiant waterfall. "They helped each other and became best friends!"

Bobby's heart warmed, feeling as if the very essence of kindness was resonating through that moment. "Sounds amazing. I'd love to hear more about it."

Adam grinned, pulling the book closer as he began to recount the tale, his words flowing like a gentle stream, inclusive and inviting.

With each word, Bobby engaged more fully, listening intently to his son as the innocence of childhood painted the narrative. He felt enveloped by the familiarity of connection as Adam animatedly described the dragon's gleeful adventures, details that tugged at his heart—he realized this was it. This was the kindness that mattered. This was the moment to embrace joy and love, bringing them further together than fate had intertwined along their paths.

As Bobby listened, the lingering shadows of his past decisions began to fade, eclipsed by the brilliance of the present. Adam's laughter rang throughout the room, bright and full of possibility, breathing life into the very air they shared. The moments of reflection had become pivotal—a harbinger of transformation, a nudge toward recognizing that his past did not dictate his future.

He placed a gentle hand on Adam's shoulder, anchoring himself to the moment as their eyes met. In that instant, Bobby understood the essence of being present—dedicating himself to becoming the father his son deserved, embodying kindness through simple acts, while allowing love and connection to flourish without the burden of regret.

The weight of experience had shifted into something purposeful and illuminating. With each passing second, he learned that the journey of nurturing their relationship was a continual adventure of exploration, one filled with vibrant possibilities just waiting to be realized. And he was ready—ready to embrace every last moment.

The Strength of Kindness

As the warm glow of the fading sun poured into their small kitchen, filling the room with a gentle golden hue, Bobby and Adam sat across from each other, the remnants of dinner still on their plates. The table, once a battleground of fast meals and hurried conversations, had transformed into an intimate space of reflection and connection. The only sounds they could hear were the occasional clink of silverware and the soft rustling of pages as Adam gently turned the weathered leaves of the Golden Book.

Bobby leaned forward, resting his elbows on the table. The slight tremor in his hands betrayed the rush of emotions that surged within him. He watched Adam's expression as he read—a mixture of wonder and deep contemplation. "You know, Adam," he began, his voice carrying a softness that had been lacking in their earlier exchanges, "just reading those stories—some of them have moved me more than I think I can express."

Adam looked up, his eyes bright with the same intensity that had drawn him into the library's depths. "There's this one story about a boy who helped an elderly man in his neighborhood. It sounded simple at first, just a kind action, but then it showed how much it meant to the man. He shared memories that changed how the boy saw the world."

"Kindness can be so simple, can't it? Yet, it holds so much power," Bobby said, as he finally felt the tide of tears welling up in his eyes. "I've realized that in my own life, I've let myself forget just how meaningful small acts can be."

Adam nodded, his brow furrowing slightly as he listened intently. "Do you remember when we didn't talk about things, Dad? When you were just working and I was just playing or studying? It felt like we were in two different worlds."

"That's why this moment feels so special, Adam. I'm grateful we can share this together." Bobby took a deep breath, trying to quell the shifting emotions within him. "At times, I was so focused on my own struggles—the painting that never seemed right, the bills, the expectations—that I forgot to look around at the beautiful moments right in front of me."

The reflection hung heavily between them. Bobby recalled the numerous days spent locked in his studio, paintbrush in hand, oblivious to his son's racing thoughts or the tender moments of shared laughter that beckoned just beyond the canvas. In the midst of his recollections, he felt a pang of guilt, wanting to fast-forward through those years where they might have missed each other so completely.

"I think we lost sight of what really mattered," Bobby continued. "Like you said earlier, kindness is something that seems so small, yet it spreads in waves, doesn't it?"

Adam smiled, his youthful enthusiasm shining through, and he responded, "Kindness is like throwing a stone into a pond; it creates ripples. The stories show how one small act can change everything."

With that, Bobby's heart swelled with a mixture of regret and admiration for the ways Adam had naturally grasped concepts that had eluded him for so long. "You're right. I remember the first time we shared a laugh over that silly cartoon. It felt like everything else faded away, like we were just... us."

Tears began to fill Adam's eyes, a reflection of the weight of their shared truths. "It's hard to believe that simple moments can have so much power. Sometimes I wish we could go back and fix everything."

"Life isn't about fixing the past, son. It's about being present now," Bobby replied, wiping his cheeks with the back of his hand. "I realize that the strength of kindness also lies in our vulnerability. It's in opening up our hearts and letting others in. I hope to do that more with you, moving forward."

Adam nodded fervently, already seeing the transformation in his father's demeanor as if a light had been flicked on in a dim room. "And I want to be more open with you, too. It's like those characters in the stories—when they share their vulnerabilities, it makes everything feel more real."

This unexpected dialogue led them both to a place of mutual understanding. Secrets, once tightly wound, opened like flowers blooming under the sun. They shared laughter coated with a bittersweet edge, reflecting on moments when they had missed opportunities to connect with each other.

Bobby leaned back in his chair, grateful for the warmth that brewed between them. "Do you remember the time I promised to take you fishing, but I had to cancel because of my painting deadline?" he asked, the guilt creeping back into his heart.

"Yeah, I do. I thought maybe you didn't care," Adam replied, his voice a whisper now.

"I did care. I still do, more than anything," Bobby corrected him, shaking his head gently. "But I let that burden overshadow what mattered most. I see that now."

Adam remained pensive, turning the pages deliberately, revealing illustrations that seemed to shimmer under the kitchen light. Each line seemed to echo Bobby's own wrestling with purpose, a constant battle between dreams and responsibilities. "The boy in this story had to confront what mattered most, too. He chose to be kind and make the right decisions, even when it was hard."

"You're learning incredibly important things, Adam," Bobby said, reassured by the wisdom bubbling forth from his son. "It's a journey for both of us."

Tears spilled freely from Bobby's eyes, and Adam's own gaze mirrored his father's; the well of emotion was profound. This moment was marked by a sincerity that fortified their bond—a healing dialogue born out of vulnerability. Kindness, they realized, was a refuge where strength and compassion resided.

"The resilience borne out of kindness shapes who we are, doesn't it?" Bobby mused, wringing his hands together as they discussed what kindness truly meant for them. This conversation, charged with revelation, marked a pivotal moment in their relationship—an anchor of sorts. "When we choose to extend kindness, we also cultivate resilience within ourselves."

Adam looked up, the light of understanding brightening his features. "It's like in the stories, Dad. Those who showed kindness became stronger. It helped them overcome challenges."

"Exactly," Bobby replied, feeling a sudden rush of hopefulness. "But it's not just about overcoming challenges. It's about nurturing connections—community." Slowly, a thought took root within him. "Maybe we could volunteer together sometime? Help others? We can take what we've learned and put it into action."

Adam's eyes widened in excitement. "That would be amazing! A chance to spread kindness... and who knows what stories we'll collect along the way?"

Bobby felt pride swell in his chest. "And think about how it can change perceptions. Communities thrive when kindness prevails. Together we'd be a ripple, creating waves that reach far beyond ourselves."

In this surreptitious unveiling of vulnerability, they had unlocked emotions imprisoned by the weight of unspoken truths. The respect they held for each other became palpable, intertwining their lives as they glimpsed the strength in their interconnectedness.

"You know, Dad, I think what you said is right. Kindness can be a bridge, one that connects people," Adam affirmed, wiping his own tears away. "We could be a part of that bridge, helping others who feel alone."

Bobby's heart swelled with pride. Adam's bravery radiated within the room. "That's exactly it, son. By sharing our stories and being vulnerable, we invite the world to join our circle. The Golden Book taught us it is essential to act upon the kindness that stirs inside us. It's like breathing."

Adam chuckled lightly. "And if we see someone struggling, we can be there, like the figures we read about."

"A guiding light for others. Kindness isn't just a single action—it can be a way of life," Bobby added, astonished by how far they had come in such a short period.

As the sun dipped below the horizon, enveloping the room in twilight, the kitchen became an oasis—a sanctuary enriched by the warmth radiating between father and son. Bobby felt lighter as they continued to delve into their emotions, each fresh tear echoing the transformation taking root within their lives.

"Do you think things can really change?" Bobby whispered, breaking the serene silence that settled around them.

Adam met his father's gaze, a revelation reflecting back at him. "I think they already are changing." He smiled, the innocence of youth merging with newfound wisdom. "We just have to keep believing in each other."

"There's undeniable strength in kindness, isn't there?" Bobby pondered, feeling the emotional weight of every word. With a nod, he continued, "It's not just about me trying to be a better father, but about us building this path together."

Together, they shared a silence that was filled with promise. In those moments, they both understood the power of what had transpired—an awakening. Kindness had emerged as a theme that bound their hearts closer, wrapping them in a fabric that grew steadily richer with each acknowledgement, each tear shed, and each story shared.

With newfound resolve, Bobby made a silent promise—to embrace each day with the same openness and willingness to connect that defined that very moment. The strength of kindness would be the cornerstone of their journey ahead, a reminder that through vulnerability and compassion, they could lift each other towards a brighter horizon.

As the shadows danced and night descended upon their home, Bobby and Adam took comfort in the shared consciousness that they were not merely wandering through life but walking a profound journey together, where kindness blossomed into resilience, love, and an unbreakable bond.

Manners through the Ages

Cultural Insights

The library's shelves seemed to shimmer as Adam and Bobby turned the pages of the Golden Book, revealing stories that transported them across the globe. Each tale unfolded like a vibrant tapestry, woven with the threads of diverse cultures, their customs, and etiquette. Adam's eyes sparkled with curiosity as he and his father ventured into these new worlds, guided by the wisdom nestled within the etched letters of the pages.

The first story they encountered was set in Japan. It painted a scene of exquisite serenity, where cherry blossoms danced in the gentle spring breeze. A young girl named Aiko was preparing for her first tea ceremony, a rite that symbolized respect and tranquility. As they read, Bobby explained the significance of each movement Aiko learned: the precise way she bows her head, the meticulous folding of the cloth, and the gentle pouring of the tea. The very act was steeped in layers of meaning, reflecting not just the importance of manners but of mindfulness and connection.

"The tea ceremony isn't just about drinking tea; it's a way of life, a moment to appreciate beauty and harmony," Bobby noted, his admiration for the intricacies of Japanese culture growing. Adam listened intently, captivated by the elegance displayed by Aiko as she interacted with her guests. The subtle nuances of bowing and the careful way she offered the tea glimmered with the essence of respect and hospitality.

As they turned the page, the Golden Book revealed another story—this time, set in Italy during a bustling family gathering. The warmth of the sun poured into a rustic kitchen, where a grandmother and her grandchildren prepared traditional pasta. The aroma wafting through the air was intoxicating, filled with love and laughter. As Adam and Bobby read about the grandmother's insistence on proper table etiquette, a new lesson in manners emerged.

"'Buon Appetito!'" Bobby exclaimed, recalling his own experiences sharing meals with family. "This phrase is more than just a way to say 'enjoy your meal'; it embodies the joy of togetherness. In Italian culture, meals are cherished moments, where conversations flow and connections are deepened."

Adam chuckled as he imagined how uncles and cousins would enthusiastically gesticulate while sharing their stories, the table overflowing with food and laughter. The grandmother's teachings reminded them both of the dignity inherent in eating together, reinforcing the idea that such rituals fortify family bonds.

Next, they traveled to Africa, where the story highlighted a young boy named Kofi who was preparing for a traditional initiation ceremony. As they delved deeper, they learned about the values of courage, respect, and community. The men of the village, dressed in vibrant garb, gathered to mentor the young boys, leading them through trials that would instill not only discipline but an understanding of their cultural heritage.

"Wow, Dad! It's like a rite of passage," Adam exclaimed, marveling at the shared atmosphere of encouragement among the village elders.

"Exactly," Bobby responded, inspired by the bond portrayed in the story. "Kofi's journey teaches us that manners extend beyond table settings; they encompass respect for one's heritage and the importance of community support." They both understood the expansive meaning of etiquette, forming a valuable lesson that transcended boundaries and echoed through generations.

As Adam and Bobby continued to turn the pages, they ventured into the vibrant streets of India. There, the story unfolded around a festival filled with colors, sounds, and joyous celebrations. A young girl named Priya prepared for Diwali, the festival of lights. Amidst the chaos, she learned the importance of greeting her neighbors with the traditional 'Namaste'—a gesture of respect that transcends language.

"Isn't it fascinating?" Bobby said, enchanted by the depth of Priya's experiences. "Namaste isn't just a greeting; it's a way of acknowledging the divinity within everyone. It's all about respect and connection." Adam nodded, recognizing how each culture had its unique expressions of kindness.

With every new story, the Golden Book transformed Adam and Bobby's understanding of the world. Through each narrative, they reflected on their own lives, considering how often they took for granted the simple act of greeting each other with genuine warmth. The lessons woven within each tale urged them to embrace a broader perspective of the values that shape various cultures.

Their voyage continued with a chronicle set in the picturesque streets of Paris, where a young artist named Christophe was mentored by an elderly painter. As Adam and Bobby read about the importance of artistic etiquette, they learned of the reverence held by artists toward each other's work, emphasizing respect and support in the pursuit of creativity. Here, manners involve acknowledging one's influences and sharing knowledge generously.

"It's like when you taught me how to paint, Dad," Adam mused. "You were always so encouraging!"

Bobby smiled, recalling the shared moments over canvases while transforming their living room into an art studio. The lessons became clear: respect for others' creativity opens doors to collaboration and growth.

Continuing their exploration, Adam and Bobby embarked on a journey to South America, where the next story introduced them to a vibrant community in Peru. They learned about the Incan celebrations honoring the earth and their ancestors. Here, manners expressed gratitude not only to fellow humans but also to nature, as villagers engaged in ceremonies to give thanks for the crops that sustained them.

"Look at how they honor their traditions," Bobby remarked, reflecting on the humility shown through their rituals. "It's all about being grateful for the small things in life."

Adam contemplated this, recognizing that gratitude became a universal principle, flowing through every culture's expressions of respect and kindness. The warmth of familial and communal bonds resonated brightly within each tale, reinforcing the notion that manners draw people together rather than keeping them apart.

As they progressed through the pages, they encountered an enchanting tale from the Arctic, where an Inuit family gathered to share stories during a long winter night. The elders' voice held authority, while the younger members listened intently, understanding the importance of narratives woven into their history. Respect for wisdom and experience echoed in the way they interacted, fostering generations of understanding and appreciation.

"This reminds me of how Grandfather used to tell stories," Adam reflected wistfully. "I should make more time to listen."

"Absolutely," Bobby affirmed, his heart swelling as he thought about the legacy of tales passed down through their family. Listening became an imperative ingredient in the recipe for connection, allowing them to honor their heritage while inviting new stories into their lives.

Finally, they turned to a story from the Middle East, where an enchanting tale of hospitality unfolded. A young boy named Amir learned the value of generosity as he and his family prepared for guests arriving at their home. The traditional customs involved preparing an elaborate feast, with meticulous attention to detail, demonstrating the essence of welcoming others.

"Inviting someone into your home is a sacred act," Bobby explained, enamored with the story's depth. "It's the core of community." Adam nodded, understanding that each of these narratives unfolded not just lessons on etiquette but intricate life philosophies.

As they closed the Golden Book, a warmth enveloped them, filtered through the collective wisdom shared throughout their adventure. Adam looked up at Bobby, the glimmer of curiosity in his eyes still alight. "Dad, can we try some of these customs? Maybe we can invent our own?"

Bobby chuckled at his son's enthusiasm, grateful for the insights fostered by their journey. "Of course! We can incorporate some of these lessons into our lives. Let's embrace gratitude, respect, and kindness in everything we do."

With a newfound appreciation for the colors of humanity they had discovered, Adam and Bobby ventured out of the library, their hearts brimming with excitement. Each culture's expressions of manners had elegantly intertwined, unveiling an intricate dance of connections that enriched their understanding.

As they left the library, they breathed in the fresh air, both feeling invigorated. Adam felt empowered to share his newfound understanding with friends, eager to create moments that honored the threads connecting all cultures.

"Maybe we can hold a 'World Dinner'!" Adam exclaimed, eyes twinkling with ideas. "We can invite everyone to bring a dish from their culture and share stories!"

"That sounds fantastic!" Bobby agreed, thrilled to see his son's enthusiasm. "It'll be a beautiful way to celebrate our shared humanity and the lessons we've learned."

With joy, they crossed their threshold, ready to embrace the nuances of etiquette that transcended borders—mysteries waiting to be shared, connections to be made, and stories yet to be told. In understanding humanity's shared values, Adam and Bobby had woven the beginnings of their own narrative—a tale of discovery, respect, and love.

As Adam drifted off to sleep that night, he found himself dreaming of cherry blossoms, pasta, and the colors of a thriving community, braiding together his experiences with a sense of belonging to a vast and beautiful tapestry. Bobby, too, lay awake, crafting in his mind the stories they would live and the manners they would embody—all bathed in the glow of the Golden Book's wisdom.

Empathy and Respect

As Adam and Bobby settled into their favorite corner of the library, the soft light filtering through the dusty windows cascaded over the piles of books they had gathered. Each one was filled with stories that promised to whisk them away to far-off lands and times, but today, they were particularly drawn to the narratives that celebrated the richness of cultural diversity.

With his heart racing in anticipation, Adam opened a book titled "The Gentle Ways of the World". The pages were filled with illustrations that danced with life, depicting people from various cultures engaging in acts of kindness and respect. The first story unfolded with vibrant imagery, telling of a boy named Ahmed from a bustling market in Morocco. Ahmed was known for his thoughtful nature and willingness to help others, whether it was carrying heavy produce for an elderly woman or sharing his lunch with a friend in need.

As they delved into Ahmed's story, Bobby noticed Adam's eyes widening with interest.

"Look at how happy he makes everyone around him, Dad!" Adam exclaimed, pointing at the drawings.

"Yes," Bobby replied, tracing the outline of Ahmed's smile with his finger. "It's inspiring to see how a small act of kindness can leave such a big impact on others. It's about connecting with people, no matter where they come from."

Adam nodded, his mind racing with thoughts about the friends he had at school. He recalled the moment he shared his lunch with Ethan, a shy boy who seemed to always sit alone.

"You know, Dad, I think sharing is like a bridge. It connects us where words might not reach. Just like Ahmed connects with people by helping them, I felt good when I shared with Ethan."

"That's a beautiful observation, Adam!" Bobby smiled, feeling a sense of pride swell in his chest. "Empathy—the ability to understand and share the feelings of another—is the bridge you're talking about. It allows us to step into someone else's shoes and see the world through their eyes. And respect? That's the foundation on which such bridges are built."

Having barely started their journey, they soon found themselves enchanted by stories of children from various cultures. A gentle peace settled over them, enveloping their hearts with love for humanity and a deep understanding of how to truly connect.

As they turned the pages, another tale beckoned them—the story of a young girl named Mei in a small village in China. Mei was faced with the challenge of understanding her grandmother, who spoke an old dialect that was no longer widely used. Adam's eyes sparkled with curiosity as he read the words describing how Mei dedicated her afternoons to learning this dialect just to communicate better with her beloved grandmother.

"She wanted to honor her grandma by learning the language she spoke, even if it seemed difficult!" Adam noted, enthusiasm pouring from his voice.

"That's right! Mei's story shows that respect is not just about acknowledging someone's presence; it's about taking the time to know their background, their struggles, and their joys. This effort strengthens not only their bond but also fosters mutual understanding between generations. It's essential to truly listen and make an effort to be inclusive, Adam," Bobby explained thoughtfully.

Adam considered this as they absorbed more stories, each rich with the emotions and customs of a different culture. They read about a young boy named Kai from New Zealand, who learned the meanings behind the Maori traditions and how they allowed him to appreciate his heritage. He realized that to defend your identity is to also honor others'.

As Bobby and Adam explored these tales, the atmosphere around them sparkled with lessons that transcended language barriers. They began to connect the dots, understanding that manners and respect varied from culture to culture but centered around kindness and empathy. Each character's journey reminded them of the intricate web of humanity, woven together through simple yet profound acts.

One story that particularly resonated with them was that of a young girl named Sita from India, who made it her mission to learn about the elderly residents of her neighborhood. Each day, she visited a different home, offering her time and a listening ear. Bobby found himself reflecting on how seldom he had taken the time to sit and listen to learn from those who held experiences and stories worth sharing.

"Don't you think that spending time with the elderly could teach us valuable life lessons?" Bobby asked Adam.

Adam's brow furrowed as he thought deeply. "Yeah! They have so many stories like that old man we see in the park. He always tells that tale about the butterfly that helped his garden bloom. Maybe I should ask him about other stories he has. He seems so lonely."

"That's a wonderful idea, Adam! The gift of listening could be one of the best ways to show respect and empathy. It opens doors to understanding perspectives different from our own and can make someone feel valued. Each person we meet has a unique life story, and by listening, we acknowledge their worth. It's something to think about when we encounter different cultures—what we share can build community and connection."

They continued through the book, diving into various encounters where empathy reshaped relationships. This led them to ponder the lessons each story illustrated—how empathy fosters respect not only among individuals but also among entire communities. The beauty of the library's tales became apparent as they learned about a boy in Kenya who built a clean water source for his village after witnessing his neighbors struggle without it. He didn't need to be reminded of the hardship, for his empathy filled the spaces of his heart, guiding his actions toward making a positive change.

"That's like Ahmed's story, isn't it?" Adam remarked.

"Exactly, Adam! Both of these boys found the courage to act out of empathy. Their respect for their communities showed how kindness has the power to inspire others, propelling change. They built stronger support systems because fine threads wove their experiences together."

As the hours slipped by unnoticed, Adam and Bobby became fully immersed in the narratives. Through laughter, bright illustrations, and heartwarming plots, they traversed continents and time, feeling the pulse of each culture as they turned the pages. Within the contours of each tale, they rediscovered their connection to each other. Each time they paused to discuss the morals behind the stories, their bond only tightened.

Amidst these conversations, Bobby began to reflect on how this newfound understanding of empathy and respect could change his own day-to-day life as a father.

"Do you think sharing kindness is hard?" he asked Adam, wanting to assess his perspective.

Adam shook his head.

"No! It's easy. It doesn't have to be big, right? Like paying attention to someone who seems upset or doing a small favor for someone who needs help. It makes people feel good."

"Absolutely! Kindness shines a light on the connections we have with others, encouraging us to slow down and appreciate those moments. Sometimes it's easy to forget, especially when life feels busy. But every small act, whether it's sharing a smile or helping a friend, builds bridges of respect, doesn't it?"

As Adam nodded thoughtfully, a sense of determination illuminated his face. Bobby dared to hope that these lessons would stick with him. Inspired by their journey through stories, he imagined himself practicing kindness daily, creating spaces for empathy to flourish in their family.

The stories in the library became more than mere escapism—they became blueprints of connection that reinforced their roles as individuals eager to bridge gaps. Bobby began to visualize how nurtured empathy could transform their experiences outside the library.

Through cultural anecdotes, they discovered unique forms of respect that often left behind lasting memories. Adam shared with his father how different communities express affection and understanding, while Bobby made mental notes to incorporate these teachings into their daily interactions.

As they explored tales of the Dalai Lama's teachings on compassion, Bobby reflected deeply on how he could implement these values into their communications. He resolved to be more conscious of how he handled his frustrations in instances when his patience wore thin while balancing his artistic ambitions and family life.

They spent hours talking, engaged in discussions that blended the grain of their lives with the richness of all humanity. What began as a leisurely visit to the library morphed into a magical expedition where empathy and respect united them across cultures. Stories shared within dusty pages became guiding stars lighting their way toward universal understanding, shaping their evolving relationship.

As they wrapped up the narratives, a shared sense of contentment settled between them. They cherished the timeless truths they had unearthed. Their reflections grew more meaningful as they stepped outside the library, eager to implement the lessons learned. Each tale lingered within their minds, weaving together a new understanding—an understanding that knowledge should serve as a bridge, opening hearts and fostering connections.

With newfound vigor, Bobby asked, "What if we made it a goal to perform an act of kindness each day this week?"

Adam grinned widely, inspired by the idea. "Yes! We could help our neighbors, volunteer at the community garden, or maybe even write letters to friends!"

Bobby loved the enthusiasm. They brainstormed ways to weave kindness into the fabric of their daily lives, each suggestion echoing back to the tales they had read. Collectively, they became excited about expanding their understanding of empathy and respect beyond mere words.

As they stepped back into their familiar world, it was clear that the connection between Adam and Bobby had deepened in immeasurable ways. They ventured forth carrying the multitude of lessons that transcended cultures, reminding themselves that empathy and respect were not just noble aspirations but keys to nurturing relationships.

As they walked home, discussing the stories that would forever echo within them, their laughter bounced off the pavement, as light and radiant as the lessons they had absorbed together. Knowing that they had embarked on a transformative journey, Bobby felt a stirring within him—a desire to elevate those values further, ensuring that wisdom from the library would be carried forward, flourishing in every step they took.

In this embrace of understanding, they cultivated an eagerness to bridge their different perspectives, fostering a home that shimmered with kindness and respect, tempering the foundation of all their interactions.

That evening, as night blanketed the world, both Adam and Bobby fell asleep with dreams brimming with new possibilities. With the glow of the day still bright in their hearts, they pictured a tomorrow filled with vibrant connections, threading kindness and respect wherever life would take them.

Everyday Elegance

In the cozy corner of the library, illuminated by the warm, golden light streaming through the tall windows, Bobby and Adam found themselves surrounded by the remnants of their exploration. The Golden Book lay open before them, its pages filled with enchanting tales and timeless lessons about manners that traversed the ages. Adam's eyes sparkled with excitement as he recounted a story he had just read about a young prince whose challenges in practicing gratitude taught him valuable life lessons.

"Did you hear how the prince learned to thank his subjects? He wrote them all letters and invited them to dinner!" Adam exclaimed, his voice brimming with enthusiasm.

Bobby nodded, encouraging his son to continue. The mundane often flourishes into something beautiful when seen through the lens of kindness. He recalled his own experiences, infused with a newfound perspective inspired by the narratives they had just encountered.

"Gratitude is a wonderful way to connect with people, isn't it?" Bobby reflected. "Seeing people's efforts—acknowledging their contributions—can make such a difference in our daily lives." He paused to remember the myriad moments where he had failed to express such gratitude, caught in the whirlwind of responsibilities and distracted by the demands of adult life. The realization stirred something profound within him.

As if sensing his father's reflective mood, Adam continued, "What if we started thanking everyone for the little things? Like, when Mrs. Hargrove hands over our groceries or when Mr. Thompson helps us tie our shoelaces at the park?"

Bobby smiled, the corners of his mouth lifting as he pictured Mrs. Hargrove's warm smile and Mr. Thompson's kind demeanor. His heart swelled with appreciation for the small interactions that often went unnoticed. "That sounds lovely, Adam. It's a great way to weave kindness into the fabric of our everyday life."

Grateful for this exchange, they decided to explore the concept of everyday elegance further. Finding inspiration, Bobby recalled moments from his childhood—his grandmother's meticulous etiquette lessons that had once seemed tedious but now unfolded with new meaning in the context of his current journey with Adam.

"Your great-grandmother would always tell me that a simple 'please' or 'thank you' could brighten someone's day," Bobby reminisced, sharing memories that felt like a bridge across generations. "She taught me that manners weren't just rules; they were little gestures of respect, creating a chain of warmth that connected us with everyone around us."

Adam's curiosity ignited. "Was your great-grandmother fancy?" he asked, envisioning a regal woman draped in pearls, elegantly sipping tea from fine china.

Bobby chuckled, shaking his head. "Not in the way you think. She wasn't a queen; she was just someone who saw beauty in ordinary moments. She appreciated the people around her, and that made her the most elegant person I've ever known. It was never about the clothes or the setting; it was all about respect for others."

Inspired by this story, Adam proposed, "Let's practice our manners today! We can start with our neighbors and see how they respond."

Bobby agreed, excitement bubbling within him. "Great idea! Let's go, and remember, it's not just about saying the right things. It's also in the way we approach people—with genuine interest and goodwill."

They began their journey by visiting Mrs. Hargrove first. As they approached her house, Adam's heart raced with anticipation. "Ready?"

"Absolutely!" Bobby said, nudging Adam forward.

Upon knocking, they didn't have to wait long before Mrs. Hargrove answered the door, her smile lighting up the entrance. "Why, hello, boys! What brings you here today?"

Adam stepped forward, nerves fluttering in his stomach. "We just wanted to thank you for always being so kind and caring when you help us with our groceries." His cheeks flushed slightly, but he held his ground with sincerity.

"Oh, my dear! That's so sweet of you to say," Mrs. Hargrove replied, her voice a soft melody. "You boys are a joy. I love seeing you every week!" Her eyes twinkled with warmth, wrapping around them like a cozy blanket.

The positive exchange filled Adam with pride, and Bobby felt a rush of gratitude towards both his son and Mrs. Hargrove. Leaving her house, they agreed to take this newfound appreciation a step further, spreading kindness like seeds across the neighborhood.

As they walked hand in hand, Bobby pointed out various details: the way the lilies swayed in the breeze, the sound of laughter from a nearby park, the low hum of conversation drifting from a garden party up the street. Every day, elegance breathed life into each moment. Each sight became amplified by the awareness of sharing them together.

Next, they meandered to the park where Mr. Thompson often volunteered to help kids learn. The old man was there, smiling as always, with children gathered around him in curiosity.

"Mr. Thompson! Hi!" Adam waved enthusiastically, breaking through the joyful energy of a story he was sharing with the group. "Can we thank you for always playing with us?"

Mr. Thompson paused mid-sentence, surprised but delighted. "Of course, Adam! I treasure our time together. You're all my little pals!"

Such acknowledgment forged an immediate, warm connection between them. Bobby watched as the children around them echoed Adam's sentiment, filling the air with laughter, a spontaneous chorus of gratitude that only deepened their bond with the community.

As the sun dipped lower in the sky, casting a soft glow, Bobby started to recognize the profound elegance underlying these simple gestures: every thank you was an invitation to acknowledge another's role in the fabric of life. His heart, once heavy with the pressures of adulthood, was now lightened with every shared smile and appreciative word.

The day unraveled into a series of interactions—stopping to thank the local librarian for her guidance or complimenting the mailman on his punctuality. Each encounter reaffirmed Bobby and Adam's understanding that elegance didn't lie within grand events but flourished in the simplicity of daily life, woven into every conversation.

Returning home, Adam recounted their day's adventures, excitement spilling over as he described the joy of noticing others and experiencing their responses. "It feels awesome, Dad! It's like we made their day better. Can we do this every day?"

"Absolutely. What we've discovered is that kindness is like a ripple. It spreads, and you never know how far it extends," Bobby replied, feeling gratitude deepen toward his son for his eagerness to embrace the world with empathy.

As evening descended, and while they settled down to dinner together, Bobby marveled at the enchanting transformation in their routines. Conversations over meals captured moments of joy and reflection, each dish symbolizing a celebration of shared experiences and kindness.

"Do you remember what the old man said about storytelling?" Bobby asked, stirring his pasta.

"Yes! He said stories connect us!" Adam replied, eagerly dropping his fork.

"Right! And isn't that what we did today?" Bobby encouraged, excitement dancing in his voice as he leaned across the table, eager to hold onto this moment with his son. "Every time we share a thank you, it builds a bridge between us and others."

As they reflected on their day, Bobby realized the change in his son mirrored a change in himself—a gradual understanding of the role they played in one another's lives. Their journey together transcended the stories from the Golden Book; it encouraged them to live out those lessons in the rhythm of their daily existence.

Days turned into weeks, and the practice of kindness wove itself into the fabric of their lives. Their routine unfolded like a delicate dance between the mundane and the profound— moments softened by politeness transformed the simplest acts into rituals that felt monumental.

One day, while grocery shopping, Bobby noticed a distressed mother struggling with her two children. Her frustration palpable, Bobby stepped forward instinctively. "Can I help you with that?" he offered, sensing her fatigue mirrored his own experiences as a parent. The woman looked up, surprised but relieved. "Oh, thank you! I just need to get this cart to the checkout."

Witnessing Bobby's kindness, Adam stepped closer, echoing the sentiment with a bright smile, "We can help too!"

As they worked together, the interaction streamlined into effortless cooperation, reminiscent of the many lessons they had learned from the Golden Book—how kindness could turn chaos into harmony, reminding them all of their shared humanity.

"Thank you, boys! You've saved my day," the mother said, her smile radiating warmth.

"Anytime," Bobby replied, the effortless kindness reflected in both their voices. As they left the store, Adam exclaimed, "We did it again, Dad! It feels so good to help people!"

His words rang true—every small act of kindness not only fostered connections but also nourished their growing bond. Life began to shift, revealing how elegance existed in the simplest exchanges—politeness began to flourish, shaping the way they saw the world and interacted with it.

The richness of their experiences began to darken the background noise caused by worry or distractions, grounding them in the beauty of present moments. Bobby felt a responsibility toward nurturing kindness within their shared environment, recognizing how it rippled forever outward.

Bobby could now grasp how each time they engaged with others, they sewn threads of manners into their lives, embellishing the tapestry of their relationship with the world beyond. They continued to bask in the glow of their shared journey as they navigated the paths of growth together, both as father and son.

One evening, while lying in bed, Adam sighed contentedly, breaking the comfortable silence. "I love practicing manners, Dad."

Bobby smiled softly, feeling a swell of affection for his son. "Me too, buddy. It's our secret to unlocking deeper connections with others."

And in that moment, he recognized the essence of elegance—not simply through the lens of manners, but as a way of modeling a life infused with kindness, weaving connections made rich through everyday grace. The journey remained alive with intention, and they felt blessed to embrace that vibrant simplicity.

As seasons changed and the fabric of their lives interwove with daily experiences, Bobby and Adam began to narrate their story into existence—a tale woven through the intricate patterns of kindness and respect, drawing upon everything they had learned through their voyage in the library and beyond.

Even in the gentlest of interactions, Bobby understood how manners were not merely behavior but rather gestures of dignity and compassion, transforming small, seemingly insignificant moments into grand experiences, resonating long past their immediate context. The world opened up before him, filled with endless opportunities to practice this art of connection, reminding him that every effort mattered.

Soon, it became second nature to pause before acting, acknowledging those they encountered, and allowing kindness to flow freely. This evolution reflected in their lives energized Bobby and Adam, transforming mundane moments into treasures where elegance inherently thrived.

In the years to come, they would look back on this foundational journey, forever grateful for the lessons gleaned from a simple visit to the library—a source where the lines of fiction and reality intertwined, illuminating the path toward appreciating each other and the beauty encapsulated in the world around them.

They began to cherish the elegance of everyday life, celebrating both their small victories and the deeper connection forged through kindness and shared experiences—a legacy of love, woven elegantly together.

A Bridge Between Generations

Conversations at Sunset

As the sun dipped lower in the sky, painting the world in shades of orange and gold, Adam and Bobby found themselves nestled on the porch of their cozy home. The air was warm, infused with the scent of blooming jasmine, which climbed trellises and hung delicately in the gentle breeze. It was the kind of evening that whispered promises of connection and reflection, a perfect backdrop for important conversations.

The day had been a whirlwind of creativity sparked by their fascinating journey through the mysterious library. They had navigated the aisles together, fueled by the contents of the Golden Book, unraveling lessons that had resonated not just in their minds but also in the depths of their hearts. Now, in this tranquil moment, they were ready to explore those lessons further.

Adam shifted on the wooden swing seated beside his father, his small legs swinging back and forth in a rhythm that had felt almost meditative. He looked up at Bobby, his wide eyes reflecting the vibrant sunset. "Dad, what was your favorite story from the Golden Book?" he asked, curiosity spilling from his lips.

Bobby leaned back, letting the swing creak softly as he pondered Adam's question. So many tales danced in his mind—each one carrying its own burdens and blessings. He could almost hear the echoes of their adventures mingling with the sound of rustling leaves. "There was one about a samurai and his unwavering honor," he began, his voice melodic in the fading light. "He faced so many challenges, and through them all, he remained a symbol of respect and integrity. It reminded me of how important it is to stay true to oneself, no matter the circumstances. What about you? Which story stood out to you?"

Adam beamed, his excitement bubbling over. "The one with the little turtle who dreamed of flying! He tried so many different ways to take off, but he always failed. But then, he built a big kite and flew high in the sky with his friends. That made me think of how sometimes it feels hard to follow my dreams, but maybe I just need a little help to soar!"

"That's a beautiful insight, buddy," Bobby replied, an emotion tightening around his heart. It was moments like these where he realized the impact their journey had forged between them, not just as father and son, but as partners woven into the fabric of life's narratives.

As shadows lengthened, Bobby felt compelled to dig deeper, to uncover more of Adam's feelings. "What makes you feel like you're struggling to follow your dreams?" he asked, careful with his words. Adam paused then, the smile fading momentarily as contemplation swept over his face.

"Sometimes, I... I worry that I won't be good enough at drawing or painting like you are. I want to make things that are beautiful and colorful, just like you did when I was little. But... what if I never can?"

The rawness of Adam's confession struck Bobby like a wave crashing against the shore, carrying with it the weight of vulnerability. He lowered himself to Adam's level, his gaze unwavering and full of understanding. "You know, Adam, there was a time when I struggled too. I didn't pick up a paintbrush and suddenly become good at it. I had to fail and practice a lot before I created something I truly liked. The key is to keep trying and not give up. Just like the turtle, you'll find your way if you keep searching for those opportunities to fly."

Adam seemed to ponder this, the light from the sunset glistening in his eyes as it flickered with the dawn of understanding. "Do you ever wonder if you're still searching for your own dreams, Dad? Like, now that you're busy being my dad and trying to paint, are you still trying to find who you are?"

A moment of silence enveloped them, a gentle pause that hung heavily in the air, filled with significance. Bobby felt a warmth swell inside—a love intertwined with pride for the thoughtful boy Adam was becoming. "Every day, Adam, I think about that. Being your dad brings me immense joy, but I also need to remember to nurture my own creativity. It's a balancing act, and sometimes one side tips more than the other. I realize now that striving to be the best for you doesn't mean I have to lose sight of myself. I want you to know that it's okay to chase both dreams—to be a kid and follow your passions while being true to yourself. Just like that samurai, I must maintain my honor by pursuing what resonates with my heart. We can all learn from these lessons together, can't we?"

The last rays of sunlight flickered low, capturing the essence of twilight's magic as day began to surrender to night. Adam nodded slowly, his brow furrowing in thought. "We can be our own heroes then, right?"

"Absolutely!" Bobby exclaimed, feeling invigorated by this shared realization. "Heroes come in all forms, not just fantastical ones or the kind we read about in books. Each day, by being courageous and kind, we become the heroes of our own stories. You're already being a hero by being brave and sharing your feelings with me, Adam. It takes a lot of courage to be honest about your dreams and fears. We can face them together."

The two fell into a comfortable silence, their eyes drifting back to the horizon. There was something remarkably profound in that stillness—a silent promise that their bond would continue to grow strong as they navigated life's complexities together. As the sun transitioned to a glowing orb, the sky transformed to deep indigos mixed with oranges; they shared the certainty that they were both on a path of understanding that linked their vast experiences—father and son—bridging generations at dusk.

As night encroached, Adam's curiosity surged once again. "What about the lessons in kindness we learned from the stories? Did you find a way to use them in your life?"

"That's a great question, Adam. Kindness is like a thread weaving its way through the fabric of our lives. Just like that samurai was honorable and just, I strive to show kindness in my actions every day. It might be small things, like smiling at a neighbor or helping a stranger carry groceries. But it's these seemingly small moments that create big ripples in the world. And you know what? Kindness has a way of returning to you, just like a circle. It brings joy not only to the one receiving it but also to the one giving it. Have you had moments where you could show kindness, too?"

Adam thought deeply. "At school, I helped a new kid who was feeling sad because he didn't know anyone. I shared my snacks with him and invited him to play during recess. We had so much fun! I didn't even think of it as being kind, Dad. I just wanted him to feel good!"

Bobby chuckled softly. It warmed his heart to hear how Adam was advocating for empathy at such a young age. "That's precisely it, Adam! It often comes naturally to you. Your heart speaks loudest when you care for someone else. You don't always need a grand gesture to show kindness. Just being there for someone, like you were for your friend, can make a world of difference. It can create spaces for dialogue and connection, just like this between us. You're still learning, but you demonstrate a beautiful sense of compassion. That's something to be proud of."

The dusk deepened, and stars began to dot the sky like shimmering jewels. The two of them fell into a contemplative silence, each lost in thought as the world around them shifted from daylight to twilight. The conversations flowed, magical in their simplicity, threading deeper layers into the fabric of their connection.

Adam leaned his head against Bobby's shoulder. "Can we make a promise?"

"Of course, buddy," Bobby replied, curiosity kindling within him.

"Let's promise to always share our dreams and fears. No matter what happens, no matter how busy we get, let's talk about stuff like this. I want to be able to tell you everything, just like you share with me."

A tear glistened in Bobby's eye, stirring within him a realm of emotions—love, gratitude, and a touch of melancholy. As he squeezed his son tighter, he could hardly express the magnitude of pride swelling in his chest. This was the essence of parenting—transforming relationships into nurturing spaces where vulnerability was celebrated and cherished.

"I promise, Adam. The way you have shared your dreams with me tonight means the world. I, too, will continue to share my aspirations, my fears, and everything in between. We are in this together, always," he assured, his voice warm and assuring.

Night had draped its velvet cloak around them as the streetlights flared to life, casting circles of illumination that danced on the wooden floor of their porch. The world hummed in a chorus of crickets and distant wind, as if echoing the promise they had just made.

With each shared conversation, they explored new realms of understanding, nurturing the fragile tendrils of connection that would anchor them through the storms of life. They illuminated each other's paths, guided by the wisdom gleaned from the Golden Book and the growing bond they nurtured along the way. Even as darkness blanketed the day, a light illuminated the space between them, one woven from love, trust, and unwavering support.

As the stars twinkled higher in the heavens, Bobby and Adam talked long into the night, crafting a narrative infused with dreams, kindness, and connection. They welcomed the soft light of the moon as it enveloped them, the certainty building in both of their hearts that these moments mattered—a bridge connecting their worlds, transcending generations and evolving with every whispered fear, every shared dream, and every promise made under the waning light of day.

Building Communication Bridges

Adam sat cross-legged on the well-used rug in their living room, a cozy space brightened by sunlight filtering through the half-drawn curtains. The room was filled with scattered toys, remnants of a day spent in imaginative play. Bobby, his father, settled across from him, an air of weariness lingering in his eyes after a long day filled with the demands of work. Yet, beneath that

fatigue, a spark of determination flickered; today was going to be different. Today, they were not just father and son—they were explorers on a shared journey, ready to traverse the uncharted territory of their emotions.

The remnants of breakfast still clung to the air, the sweet scent of pancakes mixing with the refreshing aroma of freshly brewed coffee. Bobby took a sip of his coffee, his gaze lingering on Adam, who toyed nervously with the blue strands of his Lego set. Adam's fingers danced over the blocks, a tangible representation of his creativity, yet his eyes flickered with an uncertainty that tugged at Bobby's heart.

"Hey, buddy," Bobby initiated gently, his voice warm and inviting. "What are you building?"

Adam glanced up, his expression shifting from concentration to hesitance. "It's a spaceship." He paused, a hint of pride surfacing. "But I don't know if it's going to work."

Bobby felt a pang of recognition; he, too, often felt like he was building something without knowing if it would fly. "Sometimes, it's okay if things don't turn out the way we imagine. What matters is that we create something meaningful in the first place." His own words surprised him— a simple insight, yet it resonated deeply with the narratives from the Golden Book they had shared.

Adam nodded slowly, though uncertainty lingered in his eyes. "But what if nobody likes it?"

"Then we learn from it. Every attempt is a step toward understanding. Just like a painter mixes colors to find the right shade, we learn through experimentation." Bobby leaned forward, eager to create a bridge over the chasm that sometimes formed between their generations. "You know, Adam, I've had my share of creations that didn't work out as planned. There were times I worried my art wouldn't be understood. But every stroke had its lesson."

Adam seemed to consider this deeply, his usual vibrant energy dimming slightly. "What did you do then?"

Bobby hesitated for a fleeting moment. The memories resurfaced—canvases left unfinished, ideas buried in the noise of self-doubt. "I kept going. I learned to express what I felt, not just what I thought. And that made all the difference."

The pause stretched between them, rich with unspoken fears and hopes. Bobby thought of the myriad times he had kept his feelings bottled up, fearing judgment or rejection. He was determined not to pass that burden on to Adam. "How about we practice that? I'm working on being more open, you know?"

"What do you mean?" Adam's brow furrowed, his curiosity piqued.

"Well," Bobby began, "I sometimes feel like I have to be strong for you. But being strong doesn't mean hiding how I feel. It's okay to let you see my worries and thoughts because that's real. That's authentic."

Adam's young mind seemed to process this as he toyed with his spaceship, the glow of curiosity lighting his face once again. "Like when I feel scared?"

"Exactly. When you share your fears, it helps me understand you better. I want to support you without you feeling like you have to carry burdens alone." Bobby watched as the realization dawned on Adam, like sunlight breaking through a gloomy sky.

"Okay, I'll try to share more," he promised, his voice hesitant yet firm.

"And I'll listen," Bobby assured him, feeling a swell of pride as they embarked on this new journey together. "Let's make it a practice. We'll talk openly, share our dreams and our worries—no matter how silly they might seem."

Adam's eyes sparkled, curiosity mixing with excitement. "What do you dream of, Daddy?"

Bobby chuckled softly, a smile twitching at the corners of his lips. "I dream of creating art that makes people feel something deep inside. I want to inspire others, perhaps help someone find hope when they're feeling lost."

Adam considered this, nodding with the wisdom of a child who has pondered profound things with an unclouded heart.

"Why don't you show me? We could create a big painting together!"

"A painting?" Bobby's heart warmed. He could feel the pulse of creativity igniting. "That sounds like an amazing idea. We could even make a spaceship!"

"Yeah!" Adam exclaimed, excitement bubbling over like a fizzy soda. "A giant one! With stars!"

Bobby caught the fire of inspiration in Adam's enthusiasm, recognizing the significance of their shared endeavor. Creating something together would establish an emotional bridge, solidifying their connection.

Just as the ideas flowed, so did the conversation. "So, what are your dreams, Adam?" Bobby asked, wanting to reciprocate and understand his son's budding aspirations.

Adam shifted slightly, his fingers gripping the edges of his blocks more tightly. "I... I just want to explore, like in my books! I want to go on real adventures and meet cool characters." His words spilled out, unguarded and unfiltered.

Bobby leaned in, eager to hear more. "Adventures like the ones we read about together?"

"Yeah! Like when the heroes go through forests, or into space, or fight monsters!" Adam's voice grew animated, transforming their living room into a gateway to fantastical realms. "I want to be brave like them!"

"Bravery can mean different things, you know," Bobby interjected, the thought taking root in his mind. "Sometimes, being brave is about sharing your thoughts, even when it's hard."

"What do you mean?" Adam tilted his head, confusion painting his features. He was young but clever enough to dive into deeper meanings.

"It means that we sometimes fear what others will think of us. I want you to know that sharing your thoughts and feelings with me is brave. They're precious, just like those heroes' adventures. Your dreams are important to me." Bobby's heart raced, knowing he was trying to bridge a significant gap.

The pause lingered, thick with anticipation. Adam's small face reflected contemplation, and Bobby held his breath, hoping for a breakthrough.

"I do feel scared sometimes," Adam finally admitted, his voice softer, filled with sincerity. "What if I can't be brave?"

"Bravery isn't the absence of fear," Bobby replied, recalling the wisdom embedded in the stories they cherished. "It's about how we respond to it. You can be scared, and still do the things you want to do. It's okay not to feel brave all the time."

"That makes sense." Adam's voice hinted at relief, as if a weight had been lifted. "So, my fears are okay?"

"Absolutely." Bobby grinned warmly, grateful for Adam's openness. "And I want you to know that I share fears of my own. Sometimes I worry that I'm not a good enough painter or a good enough dad." He swallowed hard, wanting to set an example by revealing his vulnerabilities, even if it felt uncomfortable.

Adam looked up, innocence etched on his face. "But you're good at it! You show me all those cool paintings!"

Bobby chuckled again, a hint of self-consciousness creeping in. "Thank you, Adam, but even the best painters struggle. I have to remind myself that it's part of my journey." He felt a sense of warmth spread through his chest as they delved deeper into this uncharted territory.

"Can I help you?" Adam inquired with surprising earnestness.

"Of course! Let's discover together," Bobby encouraged, his heart swelling with the love and connection forged in their exchange.

Their conversation danced around hopes and fears, fluttering between laughter and poignant silence, weaving into an emotional tapestry that deepened their bond. Adam shared dreams of traveling to far-off places, while Bobby unveiled aspirations that had slipped into the shadows of his heart.

As the afternoon waned, Bobby marveled at how effortlessly their dialogue turned from lighthearted whims to serious discussions. Adam spoke of wanting to be courageous, and Bobby recounted his dreams of artistic expression that still felt distant, trapped under the weight of responsibility.

"Sometimes, I feel small next to my dreams," Bobby confided, and he expected the conversation to take a more somber turn. But Adam, armed with the innocence and honesty of youth, simply responded, "But you're big enough to do it! Just like I can be big enough to be brave!"

Bobby's heart soared at Adam's simple wisdom. It reminded him that communication was the lifeblood of their relationship—a bridge enabling them to understand one another's emotions, fears, and desires more profoundly.

"Do you think we can build that spaceship with bravery, too?" Adam asked, an earnest gleam dancing in his eyes.

Bobby laughed. "Absolutely! It'll take courage to dream big and create. Just remember, we've got this together."

Their playful banter unfolded into plans to create a masterpiece that captured not just the essence of a spaceship, but also the themes of bravery and authenticity that had emerged in their discussions. Together, they envisioned a painting that reflected not only stars and distant planets but also the emotional journeys they both navigated.

"Let's make it our adventure," Bobby said, as determination kindled within him, fueled by the transformation sparked in their hearts. As they continued to share their thoughts about the painting, Bobby recognized that each moment chiseled away at the barriers that often separated them.

The evening melted into night, and as darkness draped around them, the warmth of their conversation lingered, wrapping them in a cocoon of intimacy. In sharing their thoughts and emotions, they had woven a tapestry thick with kindness and understanding. Creating a safe space allowed them to connect beyond the ordinary, nurturing a bond that proclaimed their love in layers richer than they had imagined.

"Dad?" Adam whispered as they shifted their focus back to the art supplies strewn across the coffee table.

"Yeah, buddy?"

"Can we promise to keep sharing, even when things are hard?"

Bobby's heart ached with the weight of the unbreakable bond they were forging. "Absolutely. Let's make that our promise: to always talk, no matter what."

"Promise!" Adam smiled, and in that moment, the two of them forged a bond of communication that would transcend the barriers commerce often imposed.

As they settled down to begin their masterpiece, Bobby felt a sense of relief wash over him. They were two explorers navigating the vastness of shared experiences—each brushstroke representing a step toward understanding, authenticity, and growth.

Soon, the room filled with laughter and playful storytelling woven into every stroke as they painted not only a spaceship but also a narrative of their journey. In each shared idea, they recognized the significance of their emotions, cultivating understanding between them that would undoubtedly withstand the test of time.

As the colors bled and blended on the canvas, they painted a vision that included their hopes, fears, and the promises they made to one another. Together, they crafted something rooted in love—a legacy enriched by their laughter, fears, and ultimately, their connection.

Hours passed with ease, enhanced by their growing emotional dialogue that formed the foundation for the communication bridges they sought to build. The vision turned into a narrative, binding them more tightly as they navigated through their creative venture.

"Look, it's soaring through space!" Adam shouted as he splattered a swirl of bright colors against the canvas, igniting a blend of yellows and oranges that mimicked the glow of distant stars.

"Perfect! But wait..." Bobby took a step back, his eyes darting expectantly towards his son. "What shall we name it?"

"The Brave Ship! That's perfect!" Adam exclaimed, his enthusiasm infectious.

"Then it shall be. What's our crew going to look like?" Bobby prodded, fully immersed.

"Lots of colors!" Adam replied, eyes shimmering with excitement. "And brave people! Like us!"

"Exactly! Explorers of dreams," Bobby echoed, nudging Adam playfully. "And every character will hold a piece of our story."

Their laughter filled the room, echoing off the walls like a melody of hope—an anthem celebrating their journey toward understanding and connection.

In that golden glow of creativity, they discovered not only the artistry of their hands but also the art of communication softened by time. Each brushstroke symbolized a pledge to nurture their bond, to reach out and express themselves, unapologetically navigating through emotions so they could face their larger fears together.

Bobby found that the very act of articulating emotions created a secure refuge for both him and Adam. The journey unfolded like an enchanted adventure, solidifying their love in a tapestry that would carry forward, free of doubts and miscommunication.

In the end, as they stood back to admire their collective masterpiece, an unspoken understanding gleamed between them—a glimmering connection fortified through candor and empathy, forever igniting the essence of their relationship.

"Ready for tomorrow, my brave explorer?" Bobby asked, ruffling Adam's hair softly, feeling the warmth of his son's presence glow beside him.

With a beaming smile, Adam responded, "Always, Daddy!

Always!"

As day turned to night and life ebbed into a peaceful slumber, both father and son knew they had built more than bridges; they had constructed a fortress of love, wrapped in the marvels of understanding and mutual growth.

And within that fortress, they would continue to share—a constant invitation to authenticity, weaving the fabric of communication deeply into their lives.

Strengthening Roots

As the sun dipped low on the horizon, casting a warm golden hue across their humble kitchen, Bobby sat at the wooden table, the lingering aroma of dinner wafting through the air. Adam was busy upstairs, pulling out crayons and paper, his mind concocting new worlds where heroes galloped on vibrant adventures. Yet, as Bobby gazed at the remnants of their meal—a simple stew of carrots, potatoes, and chicken— he felt a stir within him, one that beckoned him to reflect on a legacy he had yet to articulate.

His thoughts drifted back to the Golden Book, the magic that had flowed from its pages, illuminating not only lessons on manners and kindness but also unearthing wisdom that felt crucial in defining who he wished to be as a father. This was not just a record of stories; it was a tapestry—a weaving of insights that tied together the threads of history, culture, and the bonds of family.

It was a profound realization, the understanding that his interactions with Adam would lay the groundwork for the man his son would become. Each moment shared was an opportunity to instill values, to nurture roots, and to provide wings that would allow Adam to soar into the future. The task before him felt daunting. His own upbringing, marred with the chaos of incomplete dreams and half-spoken words, provided a backdrop against which this new narrative could unfold.

Sitting quietly, Bobby recalled his father's voice, sharp and occasionally fraught with disappointment. Those early lessons had not always been gentle; there were echoes of sternness that layered themselves over moments of joy. He wanted better for Adam—a softer cadence of encouragement, a background song of inspiration rather than expectation. The Golden Book had revealed to him an alternate path, a way to forge connections through shared stories that could be revisited again and again.

As he contemplated the life lessons he had gleaned from the book, Bobby envisioned creating moments filled with intention and wonder. He imagined sitting with Adam, reciting tales that resonated with their own experiences while also teaching the core values that transcended time—a kindness that reached across generations. The narratives had a unique ability to transform the ordinary into the extraordinary, rendering every lesson an adventure waiting to be explored.

The quiet of the kitchen was interrupted by the light footsteps of Adam as he bounced down the stairs, his face alight with excitement. Clutching a colorful drawing of a dragon liberating a town from the clutches of darkness, he approached his father with the uncontainable enthusiasm only a young mind could muster.

"Look, Dad! This is Captain Firebreath!" he exclaimed, spreading his arms wide as if to emphasize the heroics depicted in his creation. "He saved the villagers and their gold!" The pride in his voice was palpable, and Bobby felt a smile tugging at the corners of his mouth.

"That's incredible, Adam! I love how brave Captain Firebreath looks. Tell me more about his adventure," Bobby replied, leaning forward, eager to embrace this moment of imaginative storytelling.

With unabashed energy, Adam launched into a detailed recounting of his drawing—the village, the threat posed by a mean old witch, and the heroics of Captain Firebreath. Bobby soaked in every word, entranced by the imaginative intricacy of Adam's narrative. As the young boy spoke, Bobby found himself reflecting on how these stories intertwined with the very legacy he hoped to develop.

"Did you know that stories like these can also teach us lessons?" Bobby ventured, as Adam completed his epic with a triumphant flourish.

"What kind of lessons?" Adam asked, his brow wrinkling in thoughtful curiosity.

Bobby took a moment, carefully selecting the words that would lay a foundation for the conversation. "Well, think about Captain Firebreath. He's not just a hero because he fights the witch, but also because he helps the villagers, right? He shows kindness and courage. Those are important things we can learn from him."

The young boy nodded, his eyes wide with understanding. Bobby could see him processing this, the seeds of knowledge taking root in his mind. They were sitting at a crossroads, a moment steeped in potential that could lay the groundwork for deeper discussions of empathy, respect, and growth.

"And what about us, Dad?" Adam continued, clearly wanting to dig deeper. "What lessons do we need to learn to be like him?"

Bobby felt a swell of emotion rising within him. Here was the crux of their journey—the opportunity to translate the lessons from the Golden Book not only into words but into actions. The urge to interlink their story with echoes of the past, filtering wisdom learned into the present, sent a thrill through him.

"Well, Adam," he began, "it's about how we treat others and how we view ourselves. We can learn to be kind and generous; we can listen when someone is in trouble, just like Captain Firebreath would."

The conversation unfurled beautifully, each exchange drawing them closer as the evening continued. Adam asked pertinent questions that mirrored his youthful wisdom, and Bobby found himself searching for connections to share, weaving together bits of his own upbringing—the family gatherings where laughter mingled with the echoes of unprocessed sadness; the small acts of compassion he had observed yet struggled to emulate.

"Do you think Captain Firebreath ever gets scared?" Adam queried suddenly, tilting his head with an expression of deep contemplation.

Bobby smiled at this new angle. "Absolutely. Every hero faces fear—whether it's the witch or the thought of letting someone down. It's how we respond to that fear that truly counts. Just like we talked about courage, it doesn't mean you're never afraid. It means you choose to be brave despite that fear."

Adam absorbed this, his young mind sparking with ideas. "So, we can be brave and still be scared. Kind of like when I wanted to talk to Tommy about sharing my crayons, but I was worried he wouldn't want to play with me."

"Exactly!" Bobby said, feeling the joy swell within him as he saw Adam drawing parallels to his own experiences. It infused their conversation with a richness that made every word stand in bold relief. They were exploring feelings that transcended merely sharing stories; they were cultivating an emotional garden together.

Taking a deep breath, Bobby realized the moments they were crafting could be the defining threads that tied back to the lessons found within the Golden Book. He envisioned them revisiting those stories, much like they were crafting their own, reinforcing time-honored ideals of love, kindness, and community along the way.

"Why don't we make it a habit?" Bobby proposed, his excitement palpable. "What if every week we pick a story from the Golden Book, and we talk about it together? We can explore what it means for us and how we can relate it to what we see in our own lives."

Adam's face lit up with ecstasy, and he clapped his hands delightedly. "That would be awesome, Dad! Like our own secret club!"

"Exactly! Just you and me against the world," Bobby agreed, chuckling as he felt the warmth of connection envelop them both. It was these promises, these agreements to engage with one another, that would build the roots he so earnestly hoped to cultivate.

The evening continued, filled not merely by plates clanking and discussions of storylines but interlaced with laughter, vulnerability, and mutual affection. They allowed the unspoken bond they were strengthening to shine, edging further into the realms of dreams and aspirations.

As they settled in for the night, Bobby turned off the light in the kitchen and carried the lingering warmth of their exchange into his own world of reflection. He thought about how every lesson imparted became a seed planted in Adam's consciousness, rooted deeply throughout their time together, and each time he whispered tales from the Golden Book, they would grow into a mystical tree that could sustain future generations.

Bobby remembered his own father's fragmented legacy—an inheritance laced with rigid expectations and unfulfilled dreams. He truly wished for Adam to experience not a legacy strained under the weight of gloom but one that celebrated joy, dignity, and the strength of roots that could withstand even the strongest of storms.

As the night settled, he envisioned the productive conversations they would begin in their quest to nurture roots, imagining how each shared story would infuse their lives with color, deep understanding, and ultimately, connection. He fell asleep to the sounds of Adam's soft breathing from across the hall, feeling profoundly grateful for the privilege of fatherhood and the responsibility that brought.

As time flowed onward, the universe would continue expanding around them, allowing their roots to dig deeper as they ventured further into their intertwined destinies. Each new story would serve to remind them that the blessings of compassion must be carried gracefully forward, enriching their own lives and adding layers to the legacy they were building together.

Bobby awoke to a new day, invigorated with a vision—the time to solidify their connection to the past had come. He envisioned spontaneous adventures rooted in learning, laughter, and love that would sprout from their discussions. The first seed he planted would germinate through the infinite wisdom captured within the Golden Book, radiating the virtues of empathy and compassion through the vibrancy of their family bond.

Over pancakes adorned with syrup, Bobby felt the urge rising to suggest their very first tale. "How about we read from the Golden Book tonight?" he proposed, eyes lighting with enthusiasm as Adam poured syrup on his breakfast.

"Can we find one about friendship?" Adam asked, his curiosity unquenched.

"Of course! Friendship is a perfect place to start," Bobby affirmed, excited to explore how they could cultivate such an essential legacy together.

The day passed gradually, filled with moments woven from the legacies of past generations, invigorated by Bobby's dreams of the future he sought to impart. It became clear that within each ordinary moment lay extraordinary potential—the ability to nurture roots, share wisdom, and embrace the bonds woven throughout their lives.

As the sun set that evening, they nestled into their reading nook, the Golden Book awaiting their discovery. With hearts wide open, Bobby and Adam turned the pages together, ready to embark on the journey of connection, emotion, and growth they had unknowingly set in motion.

In the end, strengthening roots would not solely be about imparting lessons but about creating a profound legacy of love, one lined with laughter, guided by empathy, and sustained through honest dialogue. It was through this journey that they would unveil the beauty of their intertwined destinies, embracing the past while stepping boldly into the future.

Threads of Connection

Woven Experiences

As Adam and Bobby wandered deeper into the library, the atmosphere buzzed with an almost tangible energy. The flickering light overhead danced playfully against the shelves, casting shadows that shifted like memories. Each aisle seemed to breathe with stories waiting to be discovered, and every book sat quietly, eager to share its wisdom. Lost in their thoughts, father and son were connected by an invisible thread, guiding them through this labyrinth of knowledge.

"Look at this one, Dad!" Adam exclaimed, tugging at the sleeve of Bobby's coat. He pointed to a vibrantly illustrated cover hidden amidst a row of dusty volumes. Its spine bore the title in swirling, golden letters that stood out brilliantly among the mutedness around it. "It looks like an adventure!"

Bobby leaned in closer, intrigued. The title read 'The Chronicles of Eldoria,' and the cover depicted grand castles and mystical creatures, inviting any eager reader into a world bursting with imagination. It seemed to reflect Adam's delight in the stories they had been untangling together.

"Just like the stories from the Golden Book, right?" Bobby smiled as he encouraged his son's interest. They had spent long hours diving into the moral lessons found within its pages. Each narrative had gradually unfolded layers of understanding that intertwined with their own experiences, and as they shared these tales, a beautiful tapestry of growth began to emerge.

"Yes!" Adam's face lit up. "Remember the brave knight who helped the people in the village? I think he's just like the way we learned in the Golden Book about being kind!"

Bobby nodded, recalling the moment in which they delved deeper into that particular story. The themes of courage and compassion resonated within the boy as they explored how acts of kindness could shape lives. However, Bobby found himself increasingly aware of how those lessons reached beyond their linear tales, stitching fragments of understanding into the fabric of their daily lives.

"You know, Adam, as I stand here, I see our own stories mirrored in those pages. It's like we're writing our own adventure every day, but the past guides us to make better choices," he said thoughtfully, scanning the towering shelves around them.

Adam nodded enthusiastically, his mind racing to assemble the connections that threaded between the adventures in the Golden Book and the moments he cherished with his father. "And the library is like a treasure chest! It holds all these ideas ready for us!" His bright eyes sparkled as he moved down the aisle, absorbed by the titles that beckoned like silent companions.

They meandered past endless rows of books, some adorned with intricate covers and others faded and worn. Bobby marveled at the endless possibilities: classic stories of love and loss, humorous tales of friendship, and exciting accounts of daring adventures. Each book felt like a chapter in the shared narrative they crafted daily, blossoming with insights and disciplines embedded within their experiences.

As they paused to admire an unharmed chestnut, Bobby noticed something odd resting beside a colossal tome. It looked like a small, delicate piece of fabric, its edges frayed and worn, yet colorful. Curious, he picked it up, revealing it to be a handkerchief covered in cheerful patterns of flowers.

"Where do you think this came from?" he asked, examining it closely.

"Maybe it belonged to someone who read here!" Adam replied, expressing delight as he imagined a child reading stories on a rainy day when their imagination took flight.

Bobby chuckled, basking in the warmth of Adam's richly woven thoughts. "Imagine the countless stories hidden within this fabric of laughter, tears, and everything in between!" The handkerchief was not just a piece of cloth; it was a vessel carrying a string of experiences.

"And just like us, its past is woven into the present, isn't it?" Adam contributed a moment of insight, glowing in his eyes.

"Absolutely, Adam!" Bobby exclaimed, pride swelling within him. "Just like the lessons we've learned, everything has a past that informs our present. The stories we share with one another— the moments of joy, sadness, and reflection— all become threads in the tapestry of our lives. Each connection we form is a reminder that we are not alone; our experiences entwine, brightening the fabric of our existence."

The two of them continued deeper into the library, now noticing tiny glimmers within the pages of books they touched. Each heartbeat echoed with the realization that stories had followed them through the years. Together, they had shared countless moments that heavily influenced their bond.

They finally settled down on a cozy rug tucked away in an expansive reading area. Amidst towering bookshelves and tranquil surroundings, Adam took a deep breath, reveling in the serenity of their surroundings before speaking up.

"Dad, do you remember the story about the little boy who helped an older woman in the village?" Adam asked, his mind flooded with recollections.

"Of course, it showed the importance of showing kindness regardless of age—how it creates a ripple effect in the community."

"Yeah! And it made me think of the time we helped Mrs. Johnson when her fence fell down. Remember how much fun we had fixing it together?" Adam grinned, his enthusiasm palpable.

Bobby nodded, the memory coming to life vividly. They had spent the afternoon working side by side, giggling over their mismatched tools and sharing stories of superheroes overcoming their own hurdles. Just as in the Golden Book, their act of kindness transformed their day into an unforgettable adventure, while deepening their relationship with the elderly woman next door.

"That was an adventure in itself! We learned that being kind doesn't just help someone else; it makes us feel good too, doesn't it?" Bobby remarked, recognizing how their shared experience echoed throughout Adam's understanding of the world.

Adam thought for a moment before nodding. "And it also reminds us of the importance of helping others, Dad. The knight in the story helped others not only because it was right, but also because it made him strong!"

Bobby chuckled at his son's perceptiveness, reflecting on how the lessons they absorbed entwined effortlessly with their daily realities.

"Exactly! Each time we lend a hand, we add to the tapestry of joy. And sometimes, those threads can foster strength, just as you said. But it isn't just about the grand gestures—it's about the little moments, too. Always remember, kindness is like the silk thread that binds everything together."

With every conversation, they crafted new threads to strengthen their bond, sewing memories that would last a lifetime. As Bobby and Adam chatted about the adventures of the characters they'd met in books, Adam could see those tales come alive in their discussions and experiences, invigorating him in ways he hadn't anticipated.

This realization fueled a spark within him, transforming the library into an epicenter of ideas. It was a treasure chest overflowing with countless narratives awaiting to be drawn out and examined.

"There are so many stories that can remind us of things we forget sometimes, aren't there?" Adam said softly, feeling the weight of wisdom embedded in the atmosphere of the library.

Bobby smiled warmly, his heart swelling with love for his son. "Yes, my boy. These stories are echoes of the lessons we learn from life. They help us recognize that every borrowed line, every shared anecdote, builds who we become."

Adam glanced around the library, observing the colorful spines in awe. "Could we make our own story, just like the ones in the Golden Book?"

"Absolutely! We already are—every conversation, every shared memory is a thread in our story. And as we continue to connect our experiences, we weave our lives into a beautiful tapestry, much like those found in the books around us."

Being seated in that serene atmosphere, surrounded by stories and adventure, ignited a creative flame within Adam. He imagined crafting moments through dreams of heroes who fought valiantly, alongside knights and wizards, navigating challenges that mirrored their collective lives. It began to flow like watercolor across canvas, and he saw their family legacy materialize into something vivid and impactful.

Adam envisioned their next adventures while Bobby rested an arm around his shoulders. "What we build together does not happen in isolation. Our dreams are woven into the past, colored by the many stories we've encountered and lived. How exciting is that!"

In that moment, the library didn't just hold stories, it held themselves, capturing the essence of their relationship spun through adventures faced together. The minutes melted into a treasured communion, one that engraved sentiments far beyond words or shared moments. The connection was deepened as each subtle reflection tethered them to each other, reminding them that growth occurs not in solitude but through acts of companionship.

"And Dad, do you think we could come back here tomorrow to discover more stories?" Adam asked, his interest evidently piqued with a youthful zeal that bubbled over.

"Every day is an opportunity for another chapter, hanging on the threads we choose to connect through our lives. Of course, we can!" Bobby replied, laughter threading through his words.

United in both thought and spirit, father and son sprang up, energizing the rich bond they shared—their lives intricately woven together in the narrative that remained perpetually under construction. They exited the library, leaving behind a multitude of lessons entwined around their exploration like constellations shining in the dark. Their connection was their masterpiece—the stories they collected united by color and life.

And as they stepped out into the world once more, light poured over them like warm sunlight against their skin, illuminating the myriad paths before them, each one another chapter in the novel of their intertwined lives.

Fostering Empathy

As the late afternoon sun streamed through the large, arched windows of the library, the warmth wrapped around Bobby and Adam, creating an intimate space that temporarily shielded them from the outside world. The fading light cast a golden hue over the countless books that lined the shelves, their stories waiting to be unveiled, much like the feelings bubbling beneath the surface of their own exchanges.

Bobby and Adam turned towards each other, the air thick with unspoken words. It was a pivotal moment, one that held the potential to bridge their differences and deepen their connection. Both of them carried emotional burdens, and the library, with its medley of stories and whispers from the past, felt like the perfect backdrop for their conversation.

"Dad," Adam began, his voice soft and tentative, "do you ever feel... lost?" The question felt like a stone thrown into still water, rippling softly in the quiet space between them.

Bobby was taken aback. He had often hidden his struggles behind a mask of pragmatism, believing that the weight of his responsibilities should remain unspoken. But Adam's question crashed through the barrier, exposing the vulnerability he typically kept guarded.

"Sometimes, I do," he admitted, his eyes searching Adam's face for understanding. "It feels overwhelming sometimes, trying to balance everything—work, being a dad, my art. It's hard to keep track of who I am amid all those responsibilities."

Adam's brow furrowed at his father's admission. He had been preoccupied with his own life, usually focused more on his adventures in the library than on understanding the pressures on Bobby. This revelation shifted something within him.

"I thought it was just me," Adam murmured, his small hands clenching into fists. "Sometimes, I feel like I'm not good enough. Like I'm just a kid who doesn't know anything, and everybody expects me to be so much more."

The weight of Adam's revelation settled in the air, a palpable truth that resonated between them. It struck Bobby with a force that mirrored his own feelings of inadequacy.

Here was his son, navigating the world's expectations just as he had been, struggling to find his place and feel validated in an expansive universe of possibilities.

"You're more than enough, Adam," Bobby said passionately, leaning forward. "You have a beautiful imagination and a kindness that can change the world. It's okay to feel lost; it's part of growing up." Bobby's heart swelled with both pride and sorrow as he spoke.

Adam shifted his gaze to the floor, a hint of uncertainty mingling with his youthful bravery. "But what if I mess everything up? I don't want to disappoint you." His words hung there, reflecting both fear and a desire for validation that had been underscored in Bobby's earlier admissions.

Bobby felt a pang in his chest, realizing how closely intertwined their fears were. Forgotten frustrations surfaced within him: the pressure to be perfect, to grant Adam a roadmap he himself had never found. "You will make mistakes, buddy. We all do. But what's important is how we learn from them, how we rise again after falling down."

Adam met his father's eyes, searching them for certainty. This was a vital moment; Bobby had unearthed a vulnerability that came from years of balancing dreams and duties. He recognized that Adam needed reassurance, a lifeline amidst the confusion he felt at the world's demands.

"Do you promise?" Adam's voice was a whisper, filled with the raw hope that only children possess.

"Of course! I promise that I will be right here with you, no matter what happens," Bobby vowed, feeling a warmth spread in his heart as he spoke those words.

In that moment, Adam felt a shift of weight not just in his heart but in his entire spirit. The clouds that had shadowed his understanding of parenting began to dissipate. He realized that his father, too, bore his own invisible load—one that was not publicly visible but deeply felt. Bobby's struggles were almost a mirror to his own fears, and it was within this shared revelation that they began to intertwine their paths.

"Sometimes, it feels like no one gets me," Adam said, his voice softer now, heavily layered with the innocence of youth. "Like I'm just here, floating by."

"But I do get you, my boy," Bobby countered, warmth flooding his veins as he leaned closer, matching Adam's openness with eagerness. "And it took me a long time to understand that utterly. But it's essential to share these feelings, just like we're doing right now."

The library, once a vast maze of books and endless corridors, now felt cocooned in warmth where whispers of creativity breezed between them. With every shared confession, they were unearthing unexplored territories of emotional depth.

"You know, when you chase after your dreams, even if they change, it's still okay," Bobby offered, reflecting on his own artistic aspirations. "I've often expressed through my paintings, but I sometimes forget that you, too, can explore in your own way." The words flowed freely from him, full of comfort and hope.

Adam's eyes brightened. "So, it's okay for me to want to be an artist, even if it feels a little scary?"

"Absolutely! Embrace that fear, let it guide your creativity," Bobby encouraged. "And don't forget, there will be tough moments, but they help you rise even higher. Being vulnerable makes you brave."

Realizing the depth of his father's belief in him, Adam's heart swelled with gratitude. It was rare for him to feel seen, to have his weaknesses acknowledged as part of growth rather than tokens of failure.

"Thanks, Dad. I just thought, maybe, if I can't be perfect, then I shouldn't even try." Adam's honesty blended with trepidation, an emotion he had often grappled with.

Bobby shook his head slowly, his own fears intensifying in the wake of Adam's revelation. "No, perfect doesn't exist. It's about the journey, Adam. The progress—not perfection—that that makes you who you are."

They sat there for a moment, relishing in the quiet rhythm of their shared understanding. In a world that constantly demanded excellence, here they were, redefining success together.

"Do you think... I could paint too?" Adam hesitated, casting a hopeful glance at his father.

"Of course! You've got the heart for it, and that's what matters most," Bobby said, feeling a thrill of excitement rise within him as he imagined the creations that could emerge from Adam's young hands.

"Maybe you could show me how to capture moments, just like you do," Adam suggested, his eyes shining with newfound intrigue.

"Absolutely, my little artist. We'll explore that world together." The idea of sharing creative space ignited a fire within Bobby, one he had longed to ignite yet had doubted how to approach.

As they continued to talk, the contrast of their worlds—a father intertwined within adult responsibility and a child navigating the simple yet profound explorations of imagination—began to converge. Their dialogue morphed from a quiet contemplation into a celebration of dreams, fears, and aspirations alike.

"Well, what if we start with something small?" Bobby proposed. "What if we each paint something that represents how we feel right now?" A flicker of excitement sparked as he envisioned time spent alongside his son, connected by brush and color.

Adam nearly jumped at the suggestion. "I'd love that! My painting can be of this moment—us in the library, bathed in light."

"That sounds beautiful, Adam. I can picture it," Bobby encouraged, feeling a wave of pride surge through him.

"But what about you? What will you paint?" Adam's innocent curiosity blended with their earlier conversation, as he sought to grasp his father's perspective.

After a moment's thought, Bobby replied, "I think I'll paint the books themselves—the stories waiting to be told. Each one holds a piece of us, a universe of thoughts and emotions."

Their imaginations ignited, exploring the very essence of their connection through artistic expression. The boundaries of age and experience began to fade as they delved into a shared creativity, creating a tapestry intertwined with their growing understanding. The very act of engaging in art transformed their interactions, fostering a collaborative spirit that had previously felt elusive.

Tension began melting away, allowing laughter to bubble up as their conversation danced through ideas of color, techniques, and dreams. In the midst of their dialogue, a new vulnerability blossomed—a recognition that both father and son needed each other to navigate the challenges they faced, each requiring support and understanding that transcended generational gaps.

"Can we promise to keep talking like this?" Adam asked, a delicate sincerity lacing his words. "I don't want to wait until we're lost again, you know?"

"Definitely, Adam. We have to build this understanding into our lives as a routine," Bobby replied earnestly. This dialogue was not just a temporary fix; it was the seed of a new foundation for their relationship. "We'll celebrate our feelings, no matter how heavy they seem."

The prospect of open communication forged a connection, solidifying a bridge for their futures to follow. Adam, buoyed by his father's commitment, began to envision their future conversations filled with honesty, exploring emotions without fear of repercussions.

Then, as the sun dipped lower in the sky, their laughter echoed through the aisles, painting a picture of two souls connected by shared vulnerability. The library became their haven, not merely for books but a sanctuary for emotional exchange and empathy, where they could learn from one another without the shadow of judgment.

This journey together—a pursuit for understanding—soon evolved into a tapestry woven with strength and resilience that allowed them to invite not just each other's truths but also the intricacies of their individual paths. The importance of revealed emotions acted as threads, binding their experiences and enriching their bond in ways they had yet to fully understand.

In those fleeting moments, father and son had discovered an antidote to the distance that had threatened to grow between them. Their discussions morphed into profound dialogues that shaped their perceptions and invited trust into their relationship, both comforting and enlightening each other along the way.

As the library closed, shadows danced upon the shelves, while the warmth of their hearts remained bright, illuminating their paths as they prepared to venture back into the world beyond the enormous wooden doors.

Leaving the confines of stories, they stepped forward toward a future not just holding the weight of dreams, but also an awareness of each other's burdens. It was a journey laden with promise, understanding, and the remarkable strength that comes from fostering empathy.

Together, they stepped into the golden light, knowing that, no matter how difficult the outside world may become, they would face it together, knit together by threads of connection that could not easily be unraveled.

Cultivating Love

As the sun dipped below the horizon, casting warm amber hues across the library walls, Bobby and Adam found themselves seated at a small oak table tucked away in a quiet corner, away from the fading whispers of the day. The remnants of their adventure lingered in the air, and the scent of aged paper and polished wood surrounded them like an embrace. Their open hearts and minds began the delicate work of weaving connections, not just with one another but also with the essence of their shared experiences. The Golden Book lay open between them, its pages shimmering softly under the dim library light, offering more than mere stories—it had become the foundation for building something special between them.

"Do you remember the story about the kind fox?" Adam asked, his eyes alight with enthusiasm. He leaned closer, his fingers tracing the embossed illustrations on the book's pages. "The one who helped the lost rabbit find her way back home?"

Bobby nodded, recalling the tale vividly. "Yes, and how the fox taught the rabbit patience and understanding, showing her that kindness is more than simply actions—it's about being present with someone else, sharing their burdens." He paused, feeling the resonance of that lesson in their own relationship. "It's about acknowledging how our feelings can lift each other or hold us down."

Adam's expression shifted slightly; he could sense the weight behind his father's words. "Do you think that's why we sometimes struggle?"

"Sometimes, yes," Bobby replied, reflecting on their journey thus far. "I think we've both been so caught up in our own lives—the stress of being an artist for me, and your explorations of curiosity—that we forgot to focus on one another. At times, we've let life's demands pull us apart instead of bringing us closer."

Bobby could see Adam processing the depths of their conversation, his youthful mind grappling with profound emotions. He leaned back in his chair, creating a comfortable space for his son to express himself freely.

"What if we promised to be better?" Adam whispered, looking deeply into Bobby's eyes. "Like the fox promised to help the rabbit? We could make it our own adventure."

A smile broke across Bobby's face, a glimmer of hope shining through the cracks created by their misunderstandings. "That sounds like a wonderful idea, Adam. We can cultivate love—understand one another better. We can be mindful of how our actions and words shape our relationship."

"Mindfulness," Adam repeated, his brows knitting together as he thought. "Like when I take care to remember how my friends feel, even when we argue?"

"Exactly!" Bobby replied, encouraged by his son's insight. "It's about deliberately choosing to see the world from another person's perspective, letting go of anger and, instead, nurturing compassion. That's a big part of love."

As they continued weaving their conversation like an intricate tapestry, each thread they discussed seemed to solidify the bond between them even further. They recalled moments when they had fallen short of being there for each other. These instances were not merely failures but lessons—realizations that drove them to seek deeper understanding.

"Remember when I couldn't find my sketchbook?" Adam recounted, his voice now a blend of nostalgia and realization. "You were too busy to look with me."

Bobby shifted uncomfortably at the truth in his son's words. "I remember, and I regret that. I should have taken the time to help you. It was just a small moment, but it meant a lot to you, didn't it?"

Walls of defensiveness began to crumble as Bobby allowed the recollections to wash over him. Adam's honesty struck a chord, reminding him of the importance of prioritizing family. "Every moment matters, especially when it's shared, Adam."

"Can we promise to make those moments count?" The earnestness in Adam's voice tugged at Bobby's heart. "I want us to be a team. Just like the fox and the rabbit—a family that looks out for each other."

"Yes!" Bobby exclaimed, his spirit buoyed by the connection they were establishing. "We can make it a promise to help each other learn and grow—even when it's hard. Sometimes I forget that I can learn from you, too. You have so much to teach me, Adam."

The weight of those words hung in the air. Adam nodded, feeling the gravity of their exchange. "And I promise to listen more, even when I feel frustrated. We can both grow."

With every exchanged word, the seeds of kindness, empathy, and understanding were being sown, not just in abstract concepts, but as actionable commitments they could carry into their daily lives.

Bobby looked down at the surface of the Golden Book, fingers tracing its shimmering texture. "This book has brought so much to us. What if we make a habit of reading this together, discussing the stories, and sharing what we can learn from them?"

"Like a family tradition?" Adam's eyes sparkled at the prospect. "Yeah! We could even create our own stories."

"That's a beautiful idea! We can weave our own adventures, just like the ones we read." Bobby felt a swell of excitement for the days ahead. "We can write about times when we helped others or when we faced challenges and learned from them."

"What if we wrote a story about us?" Adam suggested, the creativity igniting his youthful spirit. "A story where we travel through magical lands, using love to overcome obstacles and connect with others."

"I envision us meeting characters who embody the values we're learning," Bobby added, imagining the possibilities. "We could have moments where our bond is tested, teaching us that love requires patience, trust, and forgiveness."

In the crux of their conversation, a newfound determination blossomed. With the library as their sanctuary, the whispers of the tomes began to blend into echoes of their own emerging narrative—a story steeped in love, support, and shared commitments. They were unwittingly embarking on a journey, second only to the adventures held within the precious pages of the Golden Book.

"So, the next time we have a fight or a misunderstanding," Adam proposed with youthful innocence, "we promise to talk it out, right? To remember the lessons from our stories?

"Absolutely," Bobby affirmed, feeling the warmth of their mutual commitment enveloping them like a protective cocoon. "And when things get tough, we have to remind each other that we're more than just father and son—we're partners."

They shared a moment of silence, allowing the significance of their promises to sink in. The library enveloped them in its comforting embrace, book after book echoing the sentiments they had expressed. The connection they were nurturing became palpable, a vibrant thread in the tapestry of their relationship.

As they exchanged glances, the honesty in Adam's eyes reflected sincerity and openness—a light that filled the dim corner of the library with hope. Bobby felt a wave of gratitude wash over him, cherishing the opportunity to evolve alongside his son.

"Well," Adam said, breaking the quiet moment with a giggle, "when do you think the fox finds the rabbit and they become best friends?"

"Right now," Bobby said, a soft smile curving his lips as he wrapped his arm around Adam's shoulders. "Right now is when we can start being those friends, learning and growing together."

As evening crept into night, they lingered long over conversations filled with stories, laughter, and dreams. Their hearts overflowed with newfound assurance, threading their lives with love and commitment as they prepared to navigate the path of fatherhood and childhood together.

The warm light from the library's windows faded, signifying the end of their day, yet the love cultivated between them promised to guide their own narrative long after the library closed its doors. The vision of their shared adventure awaited them, and as they stepped away from the wooden table, they held tight to their promises, an unbreakable bond forged from threads of connection that would enrich their lives, carrying them through trials and triumphs alike.

The Golden Book, a beacon through their swirling emotions, lay open, waiting to reveal more lessons, grounded in timeless themes of kindness, empathy, and love. Bobby and Adam knew that this was merely the beginning of a thrilling story—one woven through the moments they chose to share.

As they left the library, hand in hand, Adam glanced up at his father, beaming with mischievous delight, a twinkle in his eye. "Think we could find a real fox and rabbit this weekend? We could go on a real adventure!"

Bobby chuckled, his heart lighter than it had been in years, and he felt rejuvenated by the energy of his son's imagination. "Why not? Let's see what kind of mysteries we can unravel in the great outdoors."

The laughter floated into the night, their minds spinning tales of magical journeys just waiting to be realized. The path before them was illuminated by love, understanding, and shared commitments, binding their fates through a fabric unique to the bond they cherished. Together, they would cultivate love, not only through stories but through every living moment, embracing the wonders of life as they turned the pages of their own adventure.

The Realm of Imagination

Emerging from the Shadows

As sunlight streamed through the wide windows of the library, scattering glimmers of gold across the floor, Adam and Bobby felt a palpable shift in the air around them. Willing to relinquish their preconceived notions and explore the vast potential of their imaginations, they carved out a space just for themselves amidst

the towering shelves lined with books. The shadows that once confined their creativity began to dissolve, giving way to visions of wonder that danced in their minds.

Adam's eyes sparkled with curiosity as he turned to his father. "What if this very library is a portal to all the worlds of the stories we've just read?" he suggested with a mischievous grin.

Bobby chuckled, ruffling Adam's hair affectionately. "A portal? You mean like a door to a whole new universe? What would we find on the other side?"

"Well," Adam pondered for a moment, "maybe there's a world where the characters from the Golden Book live, and they're waiting for us to join their adventures!"

The concept ignited a spark of creativity in Bobby. With the sunlight glinting off a nearby desk, he placed his hands on it and leaned in, his eyes glimmering with inspiration. "Alright, then, let's build this world together," he said, his voice transforming into a dramatic whisper, as if sharing a grand secret. "Let's imagine what it would be like if we could step inside the pages of one of those stories. What adventure awaits us there?"

With that, the library transformed around them, the rows of bookshelves fading into the background of their minds. The boundaries between reality and fiction began to blur; they found themselves standing amidst a lush golden meadow filled with flowers as vivid as vibrant paint splashes, bathed in the warm glow of an endless sunset.

"Look at the colors!" Adam exclaimed, kneeling to examine a cluster of flowers, their petals shimmering like jewels. "Some of them look like the colors from your paintings, Dad!"

Bobby looked around, a smile creeping onto his lips as he admired the spectacular vista. "I think they might have drawn inspiration from the same place I do," he noted, twirling in delight. "But Adam, you did this. You guided us here with your imagination."

"Let's keep going!" Adam urged, jumping up with enthusiasm. "What do you think we'll find next? Magical creatures? Hidden treasures?"

Underneath the vivid sky, they set off together, imagining an unseen path leading them deeper into the meadow.

Suddenly, from behind a tall cluster of daisies, a flicker of movement captured Adam's attention. "Look!" he pointed excitedly, "That looks like a tiny dragon!"

The creature was indeed extraordinary—a delicate dragon, its scales glistening with iridescent hues, its wings shimmering almost like glass as it flitted between flowers. Bobby's heart raced with childlike wonder; the little dragon emitted a melodic sound that seemed to resonate with the essence of joy itself.

"Do you think it will talk to us?" Adam asked, eyes wide with fascination.

"Let's find out!" Bobby replied, kneeling to be on the same level as the creature. "Hello there, little friend! What secrets do you hold?"

To their astonishment, the dragon hovered closer, tilting its head as if to consider the questions. Then it spoke, its voice soft yet confident, "I guard the realm where imagination reigns supreme. Join me on a quest to uncover the hidden treasures within your own world."

Adam and Bobby exchanged glances, captivated by the dragon's words.

"Hidden treasures?" Adam echoed, his excitement bubbling over. "What kind of treasures?"

"Every story you tell shapes the world you live in," the dragon explained, weaving gracefully through the air as it fluttered around them. "The beauty of your reality rests in the magic of your creativity. Each treasure you find unveils a connection to imagination untold."

As they embarked on this fantastical journey, Bobby and Adam were led to a grand castle that rose majestically from the meadow's edge, constructed entirely of shimmering gold. The castle walls gleamed against the backdrop of the azure sky, and the sound of laughter floated through the air like music.

"Imagine the stories that must unfold in there!" Bobby said his artistic spirit was invigorated by the enchanting scene.

"What if we made a story together about our adventure?" Adam suggested eagerly, his eyes shimmering like stars.

"Let's start now, right here while we're in this beautiful place," Bobby replied with a grin. "You begin, and I'll follow your lead."

"Once upon a time," Adam began, taking the reins of their collaborative tale, "in a magical castle full of color and laughter, there lived a boy who loved to create. One day, he discovered a mysterious door hidden beneath a giant tapestry..."

Bobby added in with a flourish, "The door whispered secrets as he approached, promising to reveal the profound beauty lying behind it. Curiosity ignited, he opened the door, and stepped into a library unlike any other, where every book was alive with tales waiting to be told."

Their narratives intermingled, flowing effortlessly into a tapestry of adventure. They crafted intricate details about the unseen library filled with characters who danced amongst the pages, inviting heroes from every genre.

"There was a wise old woman who knew all the answers," Adam proclaimed and then moved closer to Bobby. "And a brave knight learning the art of kindness instead of just fighting battles."

Bobby nodded enthusiastically, his voice light with inspiration. "And the knight had a companion—an artistic walrus who painted the skies with colors unseen! The pair embarked on quests that taught them not just how to win but how to understand each other. Creativity became their greatest weapon."

"A weapon against sadness!" Adam exclaimed, his joy bubbling up as he imagined this new world. "And they would teach others to express themselves, too! Painting, singing, writing—everyone could be a hero in their own story."

The tales grew richer with each passing moment, layering vivid images onto their mental canvas. Imaginary scenes unraveled in a delightful cadence—a sprawling garden with flowers that twinkled like stars, rivers flowing with ink, and clouds shaped like unfulfilled dreams.

"Let's pause here!" Bobby interjected, momentarily looking around as if garnishing the scene with his artist's eye. "What if this garden holds a secret? An ancient tree that grants wishes to those who believe in the magic of storytelling?"

Adam's face lit up at the proposition. "And the tree could have golden leaves that whisper stories into the wind! But one day, it begins to lose its magic—only those who believe in creativity can restore it."

With each whispered idea, Adam and Bobby invented hidden realms and character archetypes that resonated with their own lives—their trials, hopes, and dreams intertwined with fantastical elements of adventure.

"Every time they learn a lesson about kindness, the tree blooms anew! And the dragon! He would help them discover their strengths within," Adam continued, his excitement unabated.

"A delightful twist!" Bobby exclaimed, marveling at how Adam's imagination breathed life into their narratives. "This would be no ordinary quest. It will challenge them to confront their darkest fears while embracing the friendship that grows through shared creativity."

"Right! And along the way, they would meet others who doubted their own imaginations. Together, they would show each other the beauty of sharing stories—a thousand possibilities blossoming from the simple act of creation."

The narrative wrapped around them, gently tugging at their hearts as they mixed elements of their daily life to weave together a rich tapestry of collective imagination. They discovered that in this process, their own lingering shadows-the doubts that confined their creativity—began to fade.

"Can we write down our story when we're done?" Adam asked, eyes glowing with enthusiasm. "I want to see it come alive on paper!"

"Absolutely! This will be our first tale from our adventures together," Bobby promised, feeling a surge of gratitude for this moment.

Underneath the splendor of the golden sky, they continued to explore their story, tasting each word like a delicious morsel, savoring the magic that arose from every shared thought. The boundaries of their reality melted away, and for the first time in ages, Bobby felt invigorated by the sheer power of imagination.

Suddenly, with a burst of inspiration, Adam declared, "We should have a grand celebration! Let's invite everyone we meet! The wise woman, the knight, the walrus, and even the invisible narrator who brings stories to life!"

Bobby chuckled, imagining a festive gathering amidst fields of colorful flowers, happiness abounding as laughter filled the air. "Think of the tales spun at this grand celebration—all the connections formed and lessons shared among characters from every corner of creativity!"

And so, in their minds, they began to craft an elaborate celebration filled with astounding wonders: food that sparkled, drinks shimmering like the night sky, and decorations that danced whimsically in the breeze. Characters from all walks of life fill the meadow with joy, exchanging stories and laughing over shared experiences.

As they painted their narrative with vivid strokes of imagination, Adam could feel his creative spirit strengthen each time he glanced at his father, who portrayed the very essence of excitement and joy. The shadows of apprehension and uncertainty melted away, revealing a world brimming with potential and connection.

"Maybe we are the wizards of our own creations!" Adam proclaimed, spinning around to face Bobby, his voice alive with enthusiasm. "We can conjure tales from thin air, and every time we imagine, we're building bridges to other worlds!"

"Exactly, my boy! And it's every shared experience that weaves our stories into a beautiful mosaic of life," Bobby replied, feeling a sense of urgency to nurture this moment. The bubbling joy in Adam's eyes reminded him of his own youthful dreams, reigniting a fire within—a longing to become the artist he always aspired to be. Together, they were crafting something magnificent.

With every story they envisioned, Adam and Bobby found solace in the creative act itself. Every idea resonated deeply, merging their hearts and souls as if the universe nudged them to see this journey as a calling, beckoning them to embrace the artistry that lay dormant for too long.

The sun sank lower, painting the horizon a fiery pink as they began to solidify their shared narrative, capturing fragments of adventures and whimsical elements of the characters they'd encountered throughout their journey.

Bobby felt a spark of creativity awaken within him, a sense of clarity that had evaded him for years. The act of imagination unleashed their voices, bridging the gap between a father and son, and a bond fortified through dreams and stories waiting to be unwrapped.

"Shall we write our first tale together?" Bobby suggested, capturing Adam's enthusiasm. Together, they set off toward the base of their metaphorical world, ready to carve out the foundation of their story—a project that would unearth their aspirations while rekindling their spirits.

As the shadows deepened and twilight embraced them, the contours of their adventurous narrative began to crystallize in their minds, a beautiful reminder that creativity knows no bounds. Each word held within it the key to unlocking their own truths, inviting them to forever rediscover the essence of their imaginations—and the lasting legacy of their time together.

In this magical space, father and son found solace, joy, and revelation, emerging ever so lightly from the inhibiting shadows of the mundane into the vibrant tapestry of their boundless imaginations.

Creative Adventures

The morning sun poured through the windows of Bobby's small studio, setting the room aglow with a warm, golden light. The air was thick with the scent of paint, mingled with the faint musk of old books, remnants of an archive that had surrendered its secrets to the dust. Each corner was a repository of stories waiting to be told, much like the characters Adam and Bobby had uncovered in the pages of the Golden Book.

Adam stood by the window, his eyes wide with inspiration. He was abuzz with ideas, a torrent of images flooding his mind after days of reading. The stories had painted vivid pictures in his imagination, galloping steeds, daring adventurers, and mischievous forest sprites danced upon the canvas of his mind. Just the other day, they had fought off a giant with the strength of ten men using nothing but clever tricks and a few charmed words! Now, he felt a need to bring those visions into the world around him.

"Dad!" Adam shouted, his excitement spilling over. "Let's do something! Let's create our own adventure!"

Bobby looked up from his easel, where he had been half-heartedly attempting to create a landscape that reflected his subtle longing for inspiration. "What do you have in mind, buddy?" he asked, setting his brush aside.

Adam bounced on his toes, "Let's go outside! We can use anything we find to tell our stories! You'll be the fierce knight, and I'll be the clever wizard!"

With a hesitant grin, Bobby nodded. The idea of stepping away from the easel was daunting, but he couldn't ignore the spark in Adam's eyes.

"Alright," he said, "let's see what we can conjure up."

Their first stop was the backyard, a modest area filled with an assortment of flowers, tall grasses, and a few neglected garden tools strewn about like forgotten treasures. It was a perfect setting for the start of their creative adventure.

"Watch this!" Adam exclaimed, grabbing a rusty old shovel. "This will be my magic staff!" He twirled it around, imagining it shimmering in the light of a thousand stars, a conduit of mystical power. He declared himself the great Wizard Adam, champion of the sun and protector of imaginative realms.

Bobby smiled at his son's infectious enthusiasm, picking up a fallen branch and fashioning it into a makeshift sword. "And I, Sir Bobby the Brave, shall slay all dark forces that threaten our peace! To arms!" He raised his stick triumphantly, the sunlight glinting off it as if it were made of solid gold.

As they faced each other, their hearts raced with excitement. The mundane backyard transformed into a vibrant battlefield. The flowers became enchanted forests, the air echoed with distant dragon roars, and bees buzzing in the background whispered secrets of adventure.

"We must venture forth, bold Wizard!" Bobby exclaimed, striking a heroic pose, hand on his heart, prepared to charge into the fray. "The dragon is lurking behind the wooden shed!"

"Let's go!" Adam shouted, dragging his father by the arm, both of them laughing as they made their way to the shed—their dragon's lair. They peeked carefully, breathing in through their noses, preparing for the scent of smoke and danger. To an observer, they might have appeared silly, but in their minds, they were legends.

Behind the shed, the towering sunflowers became statues of giant knights, guarding their realm. Adam imagined them wielding golden swords, their massive blooms like shields against the fierce rays of sunshine.

"Fear not, brave knight! We shall get past the guards!" Adam whispered dramatically. He pointed his magic staff toward the tallest sunflower. "A spell of invisibility!"

With a quick gesture, he twirled the shovel above his head. Bobby, fully engrossed in the game, ducked low and crept past the supposed guards. They shared conspiratorial glances, stifling their ecstatic giggles, their minds exploding with creativity.

They moved on to the other side of the garden, where a rusty old wagon lay abandoned, seemingly forgotten by time. Adam peered inside and saw remnants of gardening tools, some dust-covered potting soil, and a couple of old tennis balls.

"This can be our magical transportation, Dad!" Adam declared, jumping into the wagon without a second thought. "We can ride it into the mountains to find the magic crystals!"

Bobby grabbed a tennis ball, holding it like a gem, and climbed in after him. "A treasure beyond measure! We must protect it at all costs!" Now the wagon transformed into a royal carriage, ready to escort its passengers toward unknown worlds filled with wondrous discoveries and enchanting beings.

"Onward, noble steed!" Adam commanded, mimicking a carriage driver. The two of them steered the wagon around the garden, giggling as they bumped over uneven grass, each jolt sending them deeper into their fantastical journey. Their laughter filled the air, bright and unhindered, as they rounded a corner, the sun blazing down upon their whimsical domain.

Next, they discovered a patch of wide, flat stones that could be a treacherous bridge over a boiling lava river.

"Quickly, Wizard! We must cross before it erupts!" Bobby urged. They leaped onto the stones, cautiously making their way across. In their minds, they envisioned flames licking the edges, and they had to be swift and clever to avoid being consumed.

The stones were obstacles laden with traps, and soon one of them slipped, and both of them tumbled into a fit of giggles, imaginations spiraling into the depths of creativity.

"Great wizards can always fly over the lava!" Adam proclaimed, reigniting their adventure. "To the enchanted forest!"

"Where will we meet the Queen of All Beasts?" Bobby added, twirling his stick like a wand, thoroughly immersed in the thrilling narrative that unfolded around them.

With strong exuberance, they raced across their tiny paradise, feeling the vibrant energy surging through them, breathing life into the characters they had created. Each plant and pebble acquired a personality; each shadow played a role in the fantasy they were crafting together.

They paused near the fence, where an ancient oak tree loomed, its gnarled branches swaying gently in the breeze, providing just enough shade to add a hint of mystery. Adam pointed at it excitedly, eyes sparkling with determination. "Let's make that our castle, Dad! Every knight needs a castle!"

They both ran toward the tree, where they began stacking fallen branches and thick twigs, creating a fortress fit for a wizard and a knight. It was lopsided and haphazardly constructed, yet it bore the essence of their united imagination.

As they worked, Bobby shared tips on how to build structures, merging his practical skills into the experience. "You have to make sure the base is sturdy if we don't want our castle to collapse when the dragon attacks!" he instructed playfully, pretending to peer into the distance for imaginary foes.

"Dragons hate strong castles!" Adam replied with certainty as they continued their construction. They worked side by side, laughing, recounting their adventures and imagining the tales they'd tell.

Once their castle was complete, they sat beneath its shade, resting their hands on their knees as they caught their breath. Adam's mind was racing, still brimming with excitement.

"Dad! Now we need to create our own magic spells. What will our spells do?" he asked enthusiastically, his face lighting up with the thrill of the idea.

Bobby tapped his chin thoughtfully, "How about a 'spell of inspiration' that brings art to life? We can paint things that can talk!"

"Or a 'spell of kindness' that spreads happiness to everyone in the land!" Adam added, his imagination soaring higher than the tallest peak of their mountain.

They spent the next few hours crafting made-up spells, devising incantations and deliberately exciting rituals they would perform to cast their newfound magic. Each idea stroked the canvas of their creativity, an exciting blend of whimsical thoughts and playful antics. They wove the absurdity of their imaginings with reality—suddenly, the mundane environment around them brimmed with wonder and possibility.

Both Adam and Bobby laughed during the process, realizing how readily they could turn the simplest moments into grand adventures. They tapped into something deeper, unearthing the untethered joy of creation that had been absent in their lives. Little stones and leaves became ingredients in their whimsical spells, crafting laughter in the air—a joyous resonance that danced through the garden, echoing their newfound spirit.

As the sun began its descent, casting long shadows over their magical kingdom, they decided to pay farewell to their game for now. Sitting on the steps of their makeshift castle, tired yet exhilarated, Adam turned to Bobby, "This was the best day ever!"

"Absolutely," Bobby replied, wiping sweat from his brow. "I think we conjured some serious magic today."

They trotted back toward the house, leaving the hideaway behind for that day, but with plans simmering in their minds to revisit their magical kingdom tomorrow. The reality that their adventure had unfurled inside the walls of the ordinary filled them with newfound creativity and joy.

As they slipped into the house, Adam turned, beaming up at his father. "Can we create our own stories tomorrow?"

"Of course!" Bobby affirmed, the spark of his own childlike wonder reignited. "We could even build a moat around our castle or find a pet dragon!"

"Maybe we can invite others to join our adventure!" Adam added, eyes brimming with excitement.

"Yes, yes!" Bobby encouraged, heart swelling with the thrill of the imagination shared. "We can let them in on our spells!"

And just like that, with the fading sun framing the sky in soft hues of orange and lavender, they set the stage for countless future adventures. With imagination set ablaze, they understood that the world around them was not just a backdrop, but a vibrant canvas instinctively waiting for the strokes of creativity to be filled in—a journey fueled by their vivid understanding of stories, growth, and the potential that lay within the very fabric of their lives.

As they settled in for the evening, with tales still resonating in their minds, both Bobby and Adam realized that they had crossed a new threshold, having awakened not just the imaginations of two adventurers but unified their spirits.

Thus began their journey, navigating the realm of imagination with fearless hearts, equipped with the magic of stories and the bond of creation—an odyssey wherein each day held the promise of discovery, joy, and togetherness.

Reality Meets Fantasy

As the afternoon sun filtered through the multi-paned windows of the library, creating patches of golden warmth on the cool wooden floors, Adam and Bobby found themselves in a world that pulsed with imagination. Each shadow and each whisper of the pages became a symphony of inspiration that enveloped them, encouraging their creativity to blossom like wildflowers in spring. It was as if the spirit of the library had lifted them into a realm where reality intertwined with fantasy, and the potential for adventure stretched infinitely before them.

The two sat comfortably on a plush carpet, surrounded by an assortment of books, each one a gateway to another dimension. Adam grinned, wide-eyed with excitement, as he leaned over a book whose cover depicted a fearsome dragon encircling a glimmering castle. "What if the dragon isn't the villain? What if it's misunderstood, just like me?" he mused aloud, his mind whirling with possibilities.

Bobby felt a warmth spread across his chest, enthralled by Adam's unrestrained imagination. He thought back to his own childhood and how he had spun fantastical tales that danced within the confines of his mind. These tales had been woven into dreams of achievement, of colorful canvases and vibrant brushstrokes, but over time, they had been clouded by the weight of adult responsibilities. Here, though, in this library crafted for dreams and explorations, he felt a renewed spark igniting within him.

"What if we humanize the dragon?" Bobby suggested. "Let's tell a story from its perspective—its fears, its desires, maybe it just wants to protect its home from intruders. What if it turns out to be the hero instead of the monster?"

Adam's eyes lit up, and he nodded earnestly. "Yes! It could have a family, and it's trying to keep them safe. Maybe we can make it a friendship story where a young knight helps the dragon find its voice."

As they conceptualized their new narrative, the boundaries of reality began to dissolve, leaving in their wake a vibrant tapestry of colorful characters and magical realms. They quickly gathered loose papers, crayons, and colored pencils, forming a little workstation within the aisles of the library. With their makeshift setup, they transformed the quiet space into a creative studio.

As Bobby began to draw the outline of the dragon, he let his imagination guide his hand, sketching large wings, scales that shimmered in the sunlight, and eyes that conveyed depth and emotion. At the same time, Adam poured his heart into the illustrations of the surrounding landscape—rolling hills, lush forests, and the gleaming castle awaiting beyond.

As they worked side by side, sharing ideas and sketches, Bobby felt the pang of nostalgia for the unencumbered joy of creation that had long eluded him. The hesitations and frustrations of adult life faded into the background, leaving only the sound of Adam's laughter and the joyful interactions between father and son. The more they collaborated, the more fluidly their ideas danced together, merging reality with the vibrant fantasy they were crafting.

"Remember that time you painted the butterfly monster?" Adam asked, suddenly sparked with inspiration. "We could have the dragon turn into a butterfly at the end, symbolizing how it transformed and became brave!"

Bobby chuckled at the memory of his whimsical creature—a monstrous butterfly adorned with brilliant colors that drew both fear and intrigue. It reminded him how important it was to cultivate the art of imagination, to dance delicately between light and dark.

"Yes, just like the courageous butterflies break free from their cocoons! Our dragon could symbolize layers of fear that are shed away through friendship and understanding. It's a perfect reminder that we can also transform."

The act of creation was weaving a profound connection between them, not only in the tale they were crafting but in the very act of storytelling itself. With each stroke of the pencil, they confronted the realities of fear and vulnerability that lay hidden within their everyday lives. Adam wrestled with his insecurities at school, while Bobby found himself grappling with the daunting expectations that came with being both a painter and a father. The dragon's quest for belonging and understanding became a reflection of their own desires to navigate the complex dynamics of their relationship.

During one animated discussion, Adam paused, his brow furrowed in thought. "Do you think it's okay to be scared sometimes?"

Bobby looked over, recognizing the sincerity beneath the question. Adam's eyes held a vulnerability that resonated deeply with him. "Absolutely. Everyone feels fear at some point, even in the stories we create. What matters is how we respond to that fear. It can lead us to growth, just like our dragon. We can empower each other to face our fears, can't we?"

Adam nodded slowly, absorbing his father's words. He felt an adjustment in his spirit, realizing that both he and Bobby shared similar worries, which made their connection even more profound. The creative endeavor became more than just a story; it revealed hidden truths of their lives and aspirations, allowing them to confront emotions they often struggled to articulate.

Soon, the thrilling tales they envisioned began spilling from their lips like a gentle waterfall. They imagined epic scenes where knights rode on dragons' backs, and together they soared through shimmering skies. The illustrations evolved with each passing thought; vibrant colors danced on the pages, sparking vivid imagery that leapt to life.

"What do you think would happen if the knight at the castle realized there's no need to fight?" Bobby wondered.

"Maybe the knight has to prove that true bravery isn't about defeating the dragon, but learning to listen to it!" Adam enthused.

The exchange of these ideas sparked an unquenchable enthusiasm within Bobby; it was a reminder of the depths of creativity that lay dormant, yearning for freedom. He realized that this melding of thoughts—their conscious exploration of fantasy—allowed them to unravel the knots in their familial tapestry that were interwoven with courage, empathy, and understanding.

As the hours slipped away, the library's corners grew dimmer, kissed only by the last glimmers of sunlight that peeked through the ancient windows. They had lost themselves in a whirlwind of color and narrative, forming a realm that transcended ordinary experiences. The dragon they had created began to personify fears, perhaps echoing Bobby's childhood aspirations that once seemed so vivid yet became cloudy with time.

In a moment of spontaneity, Adam stood up, his enthusiasm bubbling over. "Let's act it out! Let's be our characters, Dad! You can be the dragon, and I'll be the knight!"

Bobby laughed at the thought. Acting out their story became a new layer of investment, allowing them deeper engagement with the characters they had envisioned. He transformed into the gruff but gentle dragon, stalling for a moment before responding. "Fear not, young knight! For I am merely a guardian!"

The two began to mirror the tensions of their imaginary world, their faces lit up with excitement as they dove headfirst into their roles. Adam brandished an imaginary sword made from a rolled-up piece of paper, charging boldly at Bobby, who gave an exaggerated roar. The library, with its towering shelves and arching high ceilings, transformed into the fantastical land they had conjured together.

Laughter echoed through the aisles, for in these moments, they were not just a father and son; they were courageous adventurers sweeping across the skies, embodying the spirits of their characters. Each clash of their playful duel revealed the lessons nestled deep within their evolving narrative—the importance of embracing vulnerability, understanding each other, and nurturing their dreams.

After several rounds of playful confrontation, Adam fell to his knees, panting dramatically. "Oh, mighty dragon, why do you guard your treasures so fiercely? Don't you see that friendship is worth more than treasures?"

Bobby, catching his breath, mirrored the wisdom of the dragon he had drawn. "Young knight, I didn't always know the true value of friendship. I was cloaked in fear, not allowing others to understand me. But perhaps... perhaps you have shown me the light!"

Their exchange became a dance of discovery, much like the stories held within the Golden Book. They realized that their adventure ebbed and flowed like the turning of a carefully crafted page, ever limitless and ever profound. Each moment was laced with joy, understanding, an acceptance of their shared experience, and a commitment to face the fears lying waiting in the shadows.

Exhausted yet exhilarated, they finally settled back on the plush carpet, surrounded by their creations. A sudden stillness enveloped them, a reminder that even amidst the wildest adventures, some truths lay quietly in waiting. Bobby turned to Adam, his expression earnest yet tender. "I often forget about the importance of embracing imagination. Today, we've created something beautiful together, haven't we?"

Adam grinned widely, the innocence of youth radiating through his smile. "Yes! And we learned that it's okay to be scared! Just like the dragon!"

With Adam's affirmation, the conversation took on an introspective tone. They began discussing the intricate layers of their lives, the aspirations they held dear, and the fears that lingered beneath the surface. Each revelation peeled back the layers of their experiences, enabling them to tackle even the most sensitive of subjects.

"I used to be afraid I wouldn't be a good enough dad," Bobby revealed, his voice lower but steady. "But I'm learning that I'm not perfect. I'm still growing, just like you. And I'm proud that we can face these things together."

Adam listened intently, feeling the weight of his father's words resonate within him. "Me too, Dad. Sometimes I worry I won't fit in at school or that I'll never be good at art like you, but when I make pictures with you, I feel brave!"

The mingling of emotions revealed a truth that had long been obscured by life's complexities. They recognized that each child must be nurtured, and even the most seemingly straightforward journey was filled with hurdles that demanded courage and a supportive hand to guide them.

In that moment, the world around them faded further, and they became two souls igniting a fire of creativity and empathy. There, amid the library's echoes, they discovered an unfathomable depth to their connection, threading through the memories of a child and the dreams of a father. Their relationship became enriched by every stroke of the paintbrush and every flick of the pencil, blurring the lines not only between reality and fantasy but also between each other's lives and dreams.

As the sun cast long shadows across the library floor, the two fell deeper into dialogue. Speaking openly about their fears became a mechanism of understanding, cultivating a space where dreams flourished freely. It uncovered uncharted territory—a commitment to embarking on a journey together, where imagination blossomed and transformed into vibrant realities.

With each conversation, they fostered a legacy of creativity that paved the way for their futures—intertwined yet distinctly individual, akin to a path emerging from overlapping dreams. Here, they could find solace in the knowledge that life's reality could be colored by their fantasies.

That evening marked a significant turn in their relationship. It became a symbol of rebirth and renewal, beckoning them toward a destiny shaped not only by burdens but also by dreams and love. As they prepared to leave the library, their hearts brimming with a narrative that would transcend mere words on a page, Adam cast a glance back at the sprawling shelves filled with forgotten tales.

"Do you think we can come back tomorrow?" he asked, full of yearning. "I want to keep working on our story! I want to know how the dragon makes friends!"

Bobby smiled, heart warmed by the initiative. "Absolutely! We'll make a promise to keep returning to our little sanctuary. After all, adventures never really end... they just transform into something new."

Hand in hand, they left the library, stepping into the fading light of the evening. With each step, the weight of reality became lighter, as both father and son embraced the beauty of their collaboration—a mosaic of dreams, fears, and most importantly, love.

And as the stars began to twinkle in the vast expanse above them, they both understood that through the power of imagination, they could navigate the intricate threads of life, weaving their experiences together into a wonderful tapestry that would last far beyond the circumstances of any single chapter.

Returning to Reality

Closure of the Journey

As the sun dipped lower on the horizon, casting a warm golden hue through the window, Adam and Bobby settled into their familiar spots on the worn couch, a sanctuary of shared thoughts and emotions. The library's mystique still lingered in their minds, but it was time to translate the enchantment of their journey into stories that needed telling. Eager to summarize their adventure, they faced one another with a shared sense of purpose, each ready to probe the depths of their experience.

"Dad, remember that moment when I found the Golden Book?" Adam began, his eyes sparkling with excitement. "It felt like the whole library opened up, like it was waiting for us to discover it."

Bobby nodded, a knowing smile creeping across his face. "I can still feel that rush, too. The moment you touched that book, something magical happened. It was as if we were both called to explore not just the stories inside but also the emotions tied to them."

Adam leaned forward, his enthusiasm palpable. "I loved how each story taught us something new about kindness and understanding. Remember the tale about the old man who helped the lost traveler? It was so beautiful! It made me want to be more like him."

"Yes," Bobby replied, his voice tinged with nostalgia. "That story resonated deeply with me as well. It was not just the man's act of kindness but also how he listened. Listening is so important, isn't it? It allows us to connect more meaningfully with those around us."

Adam nodded vigorously. "I never thought about listening that way before. Sometimes, I just want to talk, but now I understand that the best conversations happen when I really hear what others are saying."

Their exchange flowed effortlessly, like a river unburdened by obstacles. They explored the memories of the library—the silvery cockroach that had led Adam to deeper discoveries, the dusty corners filled with forgotten manuscripts, and the enchanting tales within the Golden Book that had woven their hearts closer together.

"What struck me the most about our exploration," Bobby said thoughtfully, "was how our relationship shifted throughout the journey. It wasn't just about the stories; it was about us navigating those stories together. I felt my barriers dissolving with every lesson we uncovered."

Adam's brow furrowed slightly in contemplation. "But, Dad, I think it wasn't only about the lessons. It was also about how we learned together. Like when we were discussing the importance of manners in different cultures. I felt like we were stepping into those tales as a team."

"Absolutely, buddy. That sense of teamwork made everything feel more profound," Bobby replied, his heart swelling with pride. "You know, seeing you engage with those stories taught me to appreciate the lessons I had become blind to over time. You have a unique way of seeing the beauty in things, and it inspires me."

Adam beamed at the compliment. "And you showed me that being a dad wasn't just about teaching but also learning together. I felt like I could tell you anything and that you understood."

This moment of insight hung in the air, both poignant and profound. They shared a silence, allowing the mutual realization to settle between them, enriched by the past experiences they had braved together. In that quietude, Bobby could sense the layers of their emotional journey transforming into a tapestry of trust and openness.

"It's strange how a single book can change everything," Bobby mused, breaking the silence again. "Who would have thought that dust-covered volumes held the key to revitalizing our relationship?"

Adam chuckled, amusement evident in his eyes. "Right? Books make everything feel possible. But what do you think we can take away from them? How do we apply what we learned in our everyday lives?"

Bobby leaned back, contemplating this critical question. "Well, for starters, we have to remember that our words and actions matter every day. Kindness doesn't only happen in big moments; it's woven into the small, everyday interactions. Just like the magical tales we encountered, every choice we make has the power to create ripples in each other's lives."

Adam's expression shifted to one of serious contemplation. "So, like at school, if I see someone alone, I should try to invite them to play? Or with you, Dad, I can ask how your day was, instead of just jumping into my stories?"

"Exactly! It's the little gestures that can lead to deeper connections. It's embracing empathy as a daily practice. Each day gives us new opportunities to weave kindness through our lives, just like the threads of a story. Remember when we compared our adventure to weaving a tapestry? We'll continue to add to that tapestry with each interaction."

Adam clapped his hands together. The excitement of discovery bubbled back to the surface. "I love that! Our lives are stories, Dad, and we can make them beautiful by adding those moments of kindness."

"Just like the characters in our favorite tales, we grow and learn through our experiences."

"And if we mess up?" Adam asked, a hint of worry clouding his eyes.

"That's a part of life, too. Messing up doesn't mean the story ends; it just means we have another chance to learn. We have to be brave enough to acknowledge our mistakes and mend the threads that may have become frayed. Just as the old man in the story took responsibility for his actions, we can do the same."

Adam looked down, processing the thought. "It must be hard sometimes for you to balance everything. I know you're busy with work, and it's easy to get lost. Do you think we can help each other with that?"

Bobby smiled gently, feeling the warmth of his son's concern. "Absolutely, Adam. Sharing responsibilities and experiences can lighten the load for both of us. It's about showing up for each other—whether it's helping you with your homework, or collaborating on my painting ideas, or simply being present in the moment."

"Like that time you painted the sunset with me? A day filled with laughter?" Adam reflected, grinning.

"Yes! Exactly. Those moments are like bright threads in a tapestry, too—vivid and memorable! Just like our library adventure, they remind us that even amidst our daily distractions, we can find magic in the mundane."

Adam pondered, a finger to his chin. "So, can we promise to create our moments of magic, maybe even every day? Like a little adventure?"

Bobby chuckled again, affection radiating from his every word. "I think that's a splendid idea! A daily adventure can be as simple as a walk around the neighborhood or even exploring new books at the library together. Each day can feel like its own story if we approach it with curiosity."

With renewed enthusiasm, Adam bounced off the couch, racing to peg down their goals.

As he scribbled on a piece of paper, Bobby observed with a heart full of admiration. Adam's innocent optimism was a guiding light. He saw glimpses of the bond they were weaving, filled with aspirations. The daily adventures list grew longer, now filled with everything from trinket hunts in the park to evening storytelling sessions filled with mythical creatures and self-discovery.

"And Dad! We should have a kindness jar! We can both add to it when we do something nice!" Adam proposed, beaming brightly at the thought.

Bobby chuckled, delighted by his son's contagious enthusiasm. "That's a fantastic idea! We can decorate the jar together and fill it with notes describing our acts of kindness. Over time, we can look back and reflect on how we've made our world a brighter place."

Their laughter echoed through the room as they continued brainstorming, co-creating the mosaic of their lives enriched by shared adventures. With creativity bouncing between them, imagine the stories they could craft, how they could foster kindness between themselves and others in plain sight.

In this moment, they encapsulated the essence of their journey—the understanding that their relationship would forever be transformed. Each tale from the Golden Book was a stepping stone, guiding them into the realms of the unknown. They had traveled together, discovered together, and faced challenges that would contribute significantly to their tapestry of life.

As the setting sun faded into twilight, the room dimmed, yet their spirits soared with possibilities. Each conversation served both as a reflection and a plan to build a better, brighter future infused with kindness and wisdom cultivated from their adventure. Reading about compassion had strengthened their emotional identifiers, allowing raw truths to come forth without fear of judgment. This bond had flourished through the lessons of love and patience, guiding hearts stitched through the fabric of understanding and struggle.

"You know, Dad, it feels like we've climbed this long ladder together. Every step along the way has made us who we are today," Adam noted solemnly with sincerity shimmering in his gaze.

Bobby felt emotion swell within him; pride at his son's insight filled the room with warmth. "Yes, my boy. We've been a part of a beautiful journey, one that I believe will continue as long as we both promise to keep climbing, discovering, and nurturing our connection."

"Together, we can navigate the world!" Adam exclaimed, determination evident as he hugged the piece of paper filled with dreams, ideas, and newfound promises tightly to his chest.

As they settled back into their comfortable rhythm, the warmth of their hearts illuminated the dim room, creating a sanctuary of understanding and excitement. They were not merely stepping away from the world of the Golden Book; they were transforming the treasures they discovered into a living testament of growth, solutions woven together in their daily lives.

In a world filled with uncertainties, the bond between a father and son, illuminated through their adventure, has become a beacon of hope. With every small act of kindness, they pledged to navigate the myriad of emotions and experiences that awaited them, each day a new chapter filled with warmth, understanding, and love. They were ready to return to reality, not as separate individuals but as a woven tapestry of souls, forever changed by the stories they had shared—in the library, in the world at large, and in the beautiful fabric of their lives together.

Everyday Magic

The sunlight streamed through the kitchen window, casting warm rays across the breakfast table where Bobby prepared pancakes, their sweet aroma mingling delicately with the smell of fresh coffee. The morning, once filled with the mundane duties of parenting and work, blossomed with a newfound vibrancy—an everyday magic ignited by the recent adventures he and Adam had shared in the library. As he poured the batter into the sizzling pan, he thought of how every moment now seemed ripe with potential, knitting joy into the fabric of their ordinary lives.

Adam, still groggy from sleep, bounded into the kitchen, his hair tousled and eyes wide with excitement. Today felt different. It felt brighter. It felt like the promise of something special waiting to unfold. Bobby glanced at his son, drawn to the light that seemed to flicker within him, a reflection of his own evolving demeanor.

"Good morning, champ!" Bobby greeted, his tone infused with genuine warmth. "Want to help me flip the pancakes?"

The simple question transformed Adam's sleep-laden face into a bright smile. "Yes! Let's make them awesome!" he exclaimed, jumping onto a stool and rocking back and forth like a buoyant spring.

As Bobby slid the first pancake onto Adam's plate with a flourish, his heart surged with a sense of purpose. In the past, breakfast was often just a tick on his to-do list, a necessary fuel for the day. But now, with every flip of the pancake, he was deliberately making room for shared experiences, for laughter, and for the magic of creating moments that would soon knit memories into the tapestry of their lives.

"You know what?" Adam said, delightedly stacking two pancakes high like a tower of fluffy clouds. "Let's make a pancake tower for the 'Best Pancake Awards!'"

Bobby raised an eyebrow, feigning skepticism. "The 'Best Pancake Awards' look an awful lot like a delicious trial of breakfast competition. Are you sure you're ready for the pressure?"

"Bring it on!" Adam said boldly, puffing out his chest like a heroic knight, his enthusiasm palpable. Bobby chuckled, realizing this small exchange represented a shift in their relationship—a blossoming connection where teasing became the conduit to love and understanding.

Once breakfast concluded, they decided to clean up together. Bobby plucked the last of the dishes from the table, while Adam grabbed the towel. The once mundane task of cleaning transformed into a playful arena where they tossed little bits of the leftover pancake batter back and forth, creating an airy laughter that echoed around the kitchen. Every flick of the towel and splash of water felt infused with lightheartedness and a sense of partnership that allowed them to dance around the responsibilities of life.

"Teamwork makes the dream work!" Adam announced, raising his arms in victory as they finished the last of the dishes. Bobby smiled, recognizing the wisdom hidden behind such a simple phrase. It wasn't just a neat slogan; it was an understanding they'd arrived at together, stressing the power of collaboration within their family.

As Bobby tidied up the kitchen counter, his gaze landed on a small notepad where he often scrawled down ideas for his paintings. Today, instead of blending colors or sketching forms, he wrote down a list of things he was grateful for: Adam's laughter, pancake towers, second chances, and ordinary moments styled with magic.

Later that day, the duo decided to take a walk to the park. A trip that previously folded into their calendar without much thought now brimmed with anticipation. Bobby noticed every flower that bloomed along the sidewalk, each bright color waking something deep within him.

"Look, Dad!" Adam called out, his voice laced with wonder. "That flower is purple like a dragon!"

Bobby turned to see the bold violet blooms dancing in the gentle breeze. "That could be a dragon flower," he agreed, "or maybe it's a brave little knight's flag fluttering in the wind!" Together, they crafted fanciful stories about the flowers they encountered, mingling reality with imagination in a delightful blend. With every step, the world transformed into a canvas filled with characters awaiting their stories to be told.

The park was alive with laughter, voices of children weaving through the air, painting it with joyful colors. Bobby and Adam found a bench surrounded by laughter and the sweet sounds of nature. As they settled in, Bobby took a moment to observe the families around them: parents chasing toddlers who bubbled with energy, friends tossing frisbees across the grassy expanse, and couples resting close together while whispering dreams to one another.

"This is the best park ever!" Adam declared, leaning over the edge of the bench to get a better view. "I love it here! Let's go see the ducks!"

Bobby nodded, charmed by his son's enthusiastic spirit. "Let's go. But first, how about we take a small moment to just watch?"

Hesitant but intrigued by Bobby's suggestion, Adam agreed. They sat in stillness, observing ducks gliding gracefully across the shimmering pond, little ripples tracing their path. Bobby pointed out the way the sunlight glinted on the water, mirror-like, creating a tapestry of sparkles.

"I never noticed how the water looks like a bunch of tiny stars," Adam exclaimed, his eyes wide with wonder.

"Neither did I, buddy," Bobby admitted, feeling the sweetness of their shared observation sink deep within him. The everyday magic of nature flourished around them, yet it took their new engagement, born from prior lessons, to uncover the enchantment hidden in plain sight.

"Can we come back here tomorrow too, Dad?" Adam asked, excitement bubbling beneath the surface.

"Of course, we can!" Bobby promised, feeling a rush of joy at the thought of this promised continuity.

As they ventured over to the duck pond, Bobby encouraged Adam to feed the birds. Adam giggled, oblivious to the mess he might make with the breadcrumbs, delighting in the fowl friends eager to join him for a snack. The two of them tossed pieces of bread into the water, laughing at how the ducks splashed. In that moment, Bobby felt the walls of his heart expand, embracing the essence of the simplicity that magic resided within the ordinary, to be embraced one moment at a time.

That evening, after returning home, Bobby found himself contemplating a painting. Inspired by the day's events, he grabbed his brushes, and they exploded across the canvas, swirling alongside vibrant hues and shadowy contrast. Each stroke summoned memories of the laughter shared at the park, the flurry of colors from Adam's pancake tower, and the enchantment of nature.

The smell of paint and linseed oil intertwined harmoniously, streaming through the workspace like a tangible connection to creativity he had long forgotten. It felt invigorating, a restorative force unearthing his long-neglected passion. With every brushstroke, Bobby let go of the caution that had chained him down for too long, embedding each emotional release within his art.

Adam peeked into the studio, drawn by curiosity. "Dad, that looks amazing!" he shouted, eyes wide with admiration.

Bobby grinned at his son, wiping paint from his hands. "Thanks, buddy! Want to help me add some finishing touches?"

Adam scrambled to grab a brush, the thrill of creativity igniting anew within him. Together, they spent the twilight hours turned golden with possibilities, transforming the canvas into a vibrant extension of their shared experiences, rich with the wonder they now unwittingly celebrated every day.

As the sun dipped below the horizon, painting an ethereal sky with whispers of orange and pink, they settled on the porch, sipping hot cocoa and relishing the warmth spread around them. Bobby realized that even in this simple act of sharing a drink, there lay a kind of magic that flourished amidst the ordinary—all they needed to do was be present, see, and connect.

"Dad?" Adam asked quietly, cradling his cup and looking up into the night sky. "Do you think magic is everywhere?"

Bobby smiled, savoring this moment of candid vulnerability. "I think magic exists in the moments we create, Adam. It's in the laughter we share, the kindness we show, and the beauty we appreciate in everything around us. If we let ourselves see it, we'll find it waiting for us every single day."

Adam grinned, nodding enthusiastically. "I want to find all the magic!"

"You will," Bobby encouraged, feeling a surge of protectiveness over his son's enthusiasm. "We just have to keep our eyes open."

Later that week, their routine continued to be punctuated by these moments of everyday magic. They embarked on little projects together, Adam designing fantastical drawings while Bobby painted, the sound of their laughter mingling harmoniously. Every bedtime story morphed into an exhilarating journey through the fantastical landscapes they had conjured together, a reminder of how intertwined their dreams had become.

During a rainy afternoon, they gathered scraps of paper, art supplies, and old magazines to craft a collage that visually represented their journey together—an embodiment of their emotions and aspirations, drawing from their shared adventures in the library. One by one, pieces came together until their collage took shape, vibrant and alive with energy.

"This is the best college ever!" Adam gleefully squealed, pointing out the elements that inspired him; dragons, forests, and pancake castles all fit somewhere among their conglomerate of creativity. "We should make more! Like maybe invite other kids to join us!"

Bobby paused, considering Adam's suggestions. "That sounds brilliant! We could create a whole art club right here at home."

The idea blossomed, igniting both father and son's imaginations about the potential of community and connection brought through creativity.

As days turned into weeks, the magic learned through simple moments coalesced into a vibrant rhythm. They embarked on adventures in their neighborhood, noticing tree shapes, ducks in the park, flowers blooming in front of neighbors' houses, and spontaneous community events bubbling up. Each experience was like a note in a larger melody, playing back the joyous symphony of their bond.

Bobby's interactions at work shifted, too. He reached out to colleagues more openly, making small gestures of kindness that rolled into broader ripples. The mundane meetings transformed as he brought storytelling into the conference room, sharing anecdotes about the magic of creativity that bloomed from the love he nurtured at home.

As he forged new relationships, expressions of gratitude echoed back from newfound friendships. Bobby felt alive, reassured that kindness and empathy had the power to forge lasting connections that transcended everyday responsibilities. Each step brought with it a deeper appreciation for the bonds he'd begun to explore and nurture.

One evening, after a day unexpectedly filled with joy, Bobby sat with Adam in the glow of a reassuring sunset. They reflected upon the journey they had been through since finding the golden book, each word now palpable in their hearts.

"Dad, do you think other people can feel the magic too?" Adam wondered, his brow furrowed slightly as he pondered the intricacies of their newfound perspective.

"I believe they can, Adam. But sometimes, people get lost in their own routines and forget to see the wonders all around them. That's why we have to show them, just like we learned together."

Adam nodded, his little hand balled into a determined fist. "We can inspire them to see all the magic waiting for them!"

And as they made a pact to continue noticing the beauty in every corner of life, Bobby felt gratitude welling within him—a reminder that growing together always invited magic into their existence.

As they prepared to embrace their shared dreams for the future, Bobby penned down thoughts of intention on a fresh notepad, echoing the love and understanding they had cultivated day after day.

Underneath the shimmering stars, they sealed their promise to wake up every morning and seek the everyday magic that thrived around them—magic that could be found even in the most mundane interruptions, cascading like threads of hope woven into the exquisitely beautiful fabric of their lives.

The Ladder of Growth

Reflecting on the Transformation

As the late afternoon sun filtered through the library's stained-glass windows, Adam perched on a giant wooden table, his fingers tracing the crevices of aged wood. The warmth enveloped him like a comforting blanket, shielding him from the outside world, where responsibilities danced on the edge of consciousness. Beside him, Bobby leaned back in an oak chair, his brow furrowed with a mixture of contemplation and nostalgia, reflecting on the transformative journey they had undertaken together.

"You know, it feels like we're different now, doesn't it?" Adam broke the silence, his voice lilting with curious sincerity.

Bobby nodded, his gaze drifting toward a shelf filled with books that had once felt forgotten. "It's as if we've peeled back layers of ourselves to reveal something deeper, something more genuine. The stories we've read, the lessons from the Golden Book—they've changed how I see you, and how I see myself."

Adam grinned, a spark of excitement igniting in his eyes. "Like climbing a ladder! With each step, we discover more about who we are and who we want to be."

Bobby chuckled softly, the image of a ladder resonating with clarity in his mind. "Exactly. It's like we're constructing this ladder together—each rung representing our growth, our understanding, and our bond."

They leaned closer, the shared gaze between father and son blazing with mutual recognition. In that moment, they were not merely a parent and child, but co-creators of a narrative that converged on themes of growth, wisdom, and the enduring bond between them.

"Let's think about what we've learned and how it's changed us. What's the first step on our ladder?" Bobby proposed, inviting Adam to share his insights.

"Well, I think the most important lesson for me is understanding the value of kindness. All those stories from the Golden Book showed me how little acts of kindness can create ripples, changing not just our lives but the lives of others. Do you remember the story of the wise old man and the village?" Adam's voice brimmed with enthusiasm.

Bobby nodded, a smile tugging at his lips. He recalled the tale of a man who spent his days helping villagers solve their conflicts, fostering a sense of community and empathy. "Yes, he became a bridge between people, didn't he? Taking the time to listen and understand made all the difference."

"Exactly!" Adam continued. "I realized that at times, even when I'm doing something ordinary, like talking to a friend or playing with someone at school, kindness makes everything better. It has the power to change the atmosphere, to lighten someone's burden. I want to remember that."

Bobby observed the earnestness in Adam's gaze and felt a wave of pride wash over him. He also recognized this as a critical moment in their evolution, both for Adam and in the reflections of his own path.

"That's a great starting point for our ladder, Adam. Kindness is a solid foundation. What about for me?" Bobby contemplated, allowing his thoughts to drift back through the narratives that danced in his mind.

"I think you learned to embrace your creativity again, right?" Adam retorted, his youthful eyes alive with excitement. "You've been so much more open to ideas since we started reading together! You used to be worried about not painting as much, and now you see it differently."

Bobby felt a warmth fill him as he listened to Adam. It was true; the stories had breathed new life into his artistic ambitions, which had long been set aside in favor of practicality. He had not only rediscovered his enthusiasm for painting but had allowed that passion to weave into their shared narrative, fostering creativity through their interactions.

"Yes, I'd say I've begun to see my role not just as your father, but also as your creative partner. The stories we explored shone a light on my own aspirations. They reminded me that every day can be a canvas waiting for a brushstroke, even in my parenting."

Adam leaned back against the table's edge, soaking in those words. Transformation was not merely an individual journey; it was a collective one. Their messages of growth intertwined, illuminated through stories and experiences.

"Can you remember what it felt like when we first started reading the Golden Book?" Adam asked, leaning into the moment.

Bobby let out a small laugh. "I was a bit reluctant, to be honest. I had lost a part of me—the open-minded, curious part. I saw it as more of a distraction. But as we ventured through those pages, I felt a hunger for imagination rekindle within me. I think the stories awakened a part of me that had been asleep for too long."

"And in turn, I think I started to see the world through new eyes because of that!" Adam added, his excitement bubbling. "Like a lens that made everything clearer and brighter. It taught me that growth doesn't happen in solitude—it thrives through connection and learning from each other's experiences."

The two sat in silence for a moment, letting the weight of their realizations settle between them, creating an atmosphere of deep understanding and affection.

"What was the second rung on our ladder then?" Bobby pondered.

"The importance of being open to new perspectives. I remember how you told me to absorb stories instead of just reading the words. When we approached the tale of the traveler who met people from different cultures, I learned how important it is to listen and understand other viewpoints. It's made me more compassionate towards my classmates, too."

Bobby nodded in agreement, proud of the insight that had blossomed within his son. "Yes, and being open to understanding other cultures broadens our horizons. It's about embracing diversity, isn't it? Just because someone looks or thinks differently doesn't mean they don't have valuable insights to offer."

Adam straightened, a newfound resolve sparking within him. "I want to carry that lesson with me! To be a good friend and to build bridges instead of walls. We can never be too young or too old to understand that love and understanding are universal languages."

Bobby admired Adam's passion, and for a moment, he ventured into his own recollections. "That reminds me of the time I disregarded certain opinions just because they differed from mine. I was stubborn. Shifting that mindset from rigidity to openness also serves as a reminder that everyone has a story to tell. It enriches our experience of life to learn from those narratives."

"Exactly! Our growth can be tied to the stories we've assimilated along the way. It's like each new perspective is a thread that, when woven together, transforms into something spectacular—a fabric of collective understanding and unity!" Adam's eyes sparkled with enthusiasm.

The notion of each rung and each story solidified their shared journey further; neither was an individual actor but rather part of a larger narrative. The connection deepened, threading moments of realization into the ladder they were meticulously constructing.

As they continued to talk, words filled with a rhythm of realization streamed between them. Ideas shimmered. Kinks ironed out through reflections layered with vulnerability and warmth. Bobby, diving deeper, turned the focus back to Adam. "What else do you want to carry with you?"

Adam paused before responding. "Patience! It's kind of hard sometimes, but I've noticed it's essential for everything— whether it's waiting for friends to listen to me or even for ideas to come when I'm writing stories. The tale of the tortoise and the hare showed me that willingness to take your time can lead to great outcomes."

"True," Bobby smiled, recalling the joy in Adam's face during that story. "Patience allows us to cultivate not just our thoughts but also our relationships. It's about recognizing that growth doesn't happen overnight."

As the words fell into place, Adam's expression shifted, contemplative. "I guess it also means being patient with ourselves, too, right? Sometimes I feel like I need to improve overnight in things, and it gets frustrating. But understanding it takes time makes me feel a little lighter."

Bobby felt a swell of empathy toward Adam, connected deeply with his son's sentiments. "Imagine how often we rush through our days, missing those moments that could teach us valuable lessons. Patience can transform our experiences into a rich tapestry of understanding instead of merely a race to some end goal."

They both reflected on times where, in battles of impatience, they had stumbled, where the lessons had slipped through their fingers, clouded by urgency.

"Patience will indeed serve as a strong rung on our ladder," Bobby exclaimed, moving the conversation further. The excitement of exploration filled the air as they continued their reflection. "Now, what about vulnerability? Didn't we discuss how opening ourselves up can invite connection, even if it feels daunting?"

Adam's eyes widened in realization. "Oh yes! I remember that story about the brave little girl who shared her fears without hiding behind masks. It took courage for her to be honest, and it helped her friends come together. I want to live by that example. When I'm open about my feelings, it not only helps me but brings others closer to me."

Bobby felt a warmth pool in his heart. "Vulnerability doesn't show weakness; it shows strength. It's about being brave enough to expose our true selves. Those moments of candidness can foster meaningful relationships, allowing others to feel safe about being authentic too."

As they sat there, the reflections deepened. They began to realize how intertwined their lessons had become, how each insight built upon the previous as they clutched tightly to the rungs, feeling the transformative power surge through their bond. They had, together, woven an intricate ladder reconstructing the foundation of their lives.

"What about our observations regarding creativity?" asked Bobby. "I think both of us have seen how imperative it is to let our creativity flow."

"Yes! The stories unlocked the door to a world we previously took for granted. I see things differently now, I don't have to worry about being 'perfect' or meeting standards. I can just express how I feel freely, and that in itself is a form of creativity. It makes everything lighter and more fun!" Adam exclaimed with vibrancy.

Bobby's voice deepened with conviction. "Creativity acts as a bridge to explore our emotions. If you stifle that urge, it can become a weight pressing on your heart. Our journey has shown us that nurturing creativity feeds our growth. We learn more about ourselves when we allow that flow."

They both marveled at the insights bubbling forth in the space created by their reflections. Their transformation reached heights as they delved deeper into their identities, memories, and aspirations.

"As we think about the next rung, we should address gratitude. I've felt how important it is to appreciate not just what we have, but also the experiences we've shared," Adam reflected quietly.

Bobby nodded, "Indeed. Practicing gratitude helps foster joy. If we take a moment to step back to see the bigger picture, we recognize that our journey is richer when filled with appreciation for life's intricate layers."

A warmth enveloped them as they continued to unravel these deeper connections. A sense of gratitude imbued their spirits, allowing them both to cherish those transformative tales wherein each lesson had shaped how they moved through their lives.

With each shared story, each lesson recounted, the ladder of growth stood tall, reaching higher towards hopes and dreams yet to be fulfilled. The light streaming in through the windows illuminated the path ahead, shining brightly upon their steps and emphasizing renewed purpose.

"What if we also consider forgiveness as part of our ladder? I remember how forgiveness in the story about the knights and dragons shaped their beliefs about trust and acceptance," Adam reminisced.

Bobby smiled knowingly. "The bravery it takes to forgive takes strength. It's not always easy, but letting go liberates us from resentment. Exploring the value of forgiveness empowers us to rebuild trust, whether it's with ourselves or with those we've grown distant from."

Reflecting on the richness of their dialogues, Adam felt the weight of his father's words sink in. He recognized that forgiveness had the power to mend fractures, allowing for unity in their familial bonds.

"So, almost everything is interlinked, right? Each rung, each lesson connects to the others?" Adam pondered, constructing those connections in his mind.

Bobby leaned in closer, admiration resonating through him. "Precisely. Each lesson we encompass doesn't just stand alone; it becomes the fabric of our growth. We build resilience through understanding. When we examine our journey, we can see how intertwined all of these concepts really are, forming the very essence of our character."

In that immersive moment of connection, the air stirred with magic, sculpting an ambiance that embraced their shared laughter and meaningful conversations.

"Let's not forget the importance of joy in our journey," Bobby suggested. "Finding joy in little things makes the entirety of our experience richer. It keeps our hearts open and our spirits buoyant."

Adam chuckled, nodding fervently. "I've learned that joy can come without a grand motive; even the smallest moments can turn our day around!"

"Yes, joy colors our experiences. It fills the empty spaces with love and laughter, reminding us to appreciate the journey just as much as the destination." Bobby's affirmation echoed through them, enriching their bond.

As they structured their ladder, adding rungs that echoed hope and confidence, they found themselves brimming with enthusiasm, encouraging one another to climb ever higher.

With every shared experience, with every lesson learned, their journey became a vivid tapestry that transcended into the realm of the extraordinary. Through whatever challenges lay ahead, they had become more equipped to face life, hand in hand, bound by love and an understanding that transcended words.

With the image of the ladder firmly in their minds, they exchanged knowing glances, each committed to scaling the heights together. Adam felt a swell of appreciation for the magical bond they shared. He understood now that the journey of transformation was merely beginning, each story unfolding richer than the last and inked upon the pages of their lives.

The space between them felt sacred, alive with possibility. As they navigated their emotions and aspirations, they reinforced the strength of their relationship, vitalizing their spirits, encouraging one another through imagination and understanding. In that moment, no dream felt too far, no aspiration too grand. They were ready to embrace the journey ahead, together.

Promises for the Future

As the last light of day dipped below the horizon, painting the sky with hues of orange and lavender, Adam and Bobby sat side by side on the porch of their modest home, the warm breeze wrapping around them like a soft blanket. The echoes of their recent adventures in the library whispered through the air, intertwining with their newfound commitments. They had traveled through realms unknown and returned, richer not just in knowledge but in understanding of each other.

"Dad, do you think the stories we read will always be with us?" Adam asked, his voice still carrying the wonder of the countless tales they had uncovered. The evening light danced in his eyes, reflecting curiosity and innocence, traits that warmed Bobby's heart.

Bobby chuckled softly, taking a moment to gather his thoughts. "I like to think so, Adam. Stories have a way of sticking with us, shaping who we are. Just like the lessons in the Golden Book, they become part of the fabric of our lives. What about you? Do you believe they're impactful?"

With a thoughtful expression, Adam nodded vigorously. "Yes! They've taught me so much about kindness. I want to be like the heroes in the stories, making good choices and being brave. And I want to share these lessons with everyone!"

Bobby felt a rush of pride, his chest swelling at Adam's words. Encouraging his son's curiosity had always been one of his deepest desires. Yet, as he listened to Adam's earnest proclamations, he realized how much he, too, had grown throughout their journey.

"Your heart is already so big," Bobby replied, gazing at their garden, where fireflies began to emerge, dotting the twilight with flickers of light. "Finding ways to share kindness is a noble aspiration. It's something we can promise to do together. How about we start making those promises?"

Adam's face lit up, as if the very stars had joined the conversation. "Yes! Let's make promises! Like our own secret pact!"

"Yes, a pact!" Bobby agreed, his heart glowing with anticipation. "Let's talk about what we want for our future, things that will keep our bond strong."

In that moment, beneath the tapestry of the cosmos, they began carving out the essence of their future. Adam took a deep breath before speaking, the night wrapping around him like a cloak of confidence. "Promise me you'll always listen to me when I have a story to share. I want to tell you everything!"

Bobby nodded solemnly. "I promise, Adam. I might not always have the time, but I will always make time for your stories. You matter to me, and so do your thoughts."

"Really?" Adam asked, his voice tinged with disbelief and hope.

"Really, really," Bobby replied, a smile spreading across his face. "And I promise to share my own stories and dreams with you. I want you to know what inspires me as well. We can learn from each other."

As the weight of the promise settled between them like a palpable thread, Adam's eyes sparkled with joy. "And let's promise to be kind, even when things are hard!" His earnestness was infectious.

Bobby raised an eyebrow, impressed. "That's a wonderful addition. Things can get tough, but we will always remember to step into each other's shoes first."

"Right! And no mean words, either!" Adam chimed in, his resolve mounting. "We'll remember the Golden Book, how kindness changes everything. We'll practice that, won't we?"

Bobby chuckled again, a soft sound against the backdrop of rustling leaves. "Definitely. Kindness first." He paused, contemplating the essence of Adam's words. The journey they took through the library echoed with memories of unlearning old habits, learning new ones, and each tale imparting the importance of empathy in their interactions. "We'll support each other whenever we can. If you're struggling, I promise to help you. Just as I hope you'll help me when I'm lost."

"I will!" Adam promised fervently, his small hand forming a fist in joy. "And we can have adventures too, right? Like exploring more libraries or finding new books to read!" His enthusiasm was infectious, wrapping around Bobby like a buoyant wave of optimism.

"Yes, we can absolutely do that!" Bobby exclaimed, feeling the remnants of his creative spirit reignite at Adam's zest for exploration. "Let's make a list of places we want to visit—museums, parks, even different countries someday. As long as we learn and do it together, it doesn't matter where we go."

"Can we go to Japan?" Adam asked with wide eyes, the sparkle of adventure illuminating his features.

Bobby smiled, momentarily caught in dreams woven from stories of cherry blossoms and ancient temples. "That's certainly possible! We can explore cultures and their stories. You can teach me what you learn about their manners, and I'll share my artistic visions too."

The concept of intertwining their aspirations deepened a bond that had once rested on tentative grounds. This promise of exploration reignited Bobby's own artistic inclinations, creating a ripple of excitement as they began to see the world through the lens of learners eager to grow.

"Let's not just promise to go places," Adam continued, a new thought dawning upon him. "Let's promise to help each other create new things! Like stories or paintings." He gestured animatedly, his creativity bubbling forth. "We can have our own art nights!"

"Absolutely!" Bobby exclaimed, fully caught up in the dreamlike fervor. "We can dedicate nights to create. Maybe we'll even have a gallery of our own one day! An exhibition showcasing our adventures!"

With each promise woven from heartfelt aspirations, Adam and Bobby began mapping out a life interlaced with creativity, adventure, and empathy. As the sky darkened above them, they painted futures brightly, both expressing individual hopes while still nurturing their connection.

"I want us to promise to forgive each other, too," Adam added, his earnest nature shining. "Sometimes, I might mess up or get frustrated, and I know you will too. Let's always promise we will forgive each other and talk it through. Like in those stories, when characters learn from their mistakes."

Bobby felt a weight lift from his heart at Adam's wisdom. "That's a crucial promise. Forgiveness will keep our bond strong, no matter how far we grow. And I promise to always communicate openly about my mistakes, too."

In that sacred exchange, their dialogue became more than just aspirations—it became a foundation upon which to relate and navigate through life's challenges.

"Can we also promise to explore our imaginations?" Adam added, his youthful spirit glowing with possibility. "Like inventing games, or being silly when we want to? Not being afraid to create magic all around us."

"Yes!" Bobby agreed wholeheartedly. "That's vital. In the midst of our busy lives, we must promise to set aside time for imagination—time to create magic in the mundane. We'll delve into every moment."

"Okay!" Adam beamed. "And let's promise to be each other's biggest supporters, so we always feel brave while trying new things! Like painting and writing and all the dreams we chase!"

Bobby's heart swelled with pride. "Of course. Your dreams are mine, and I'll encourage you to chase them as fiercely as I pursue my own passions. In return, I'll cherish you supporting mine." Adam's infectious enthusiasm spread warmth throughout the cool evening air, wrapping it in the golden glow of familial love.

"And we'll promise to help others, too—like the values we learned from all those stories," Adam stated, his innocence grounded in the wisdom he had absorbed. "It's important to share everything—kindness, creativity, and dreams. We can be a part of other people's stories, too."

"Beautifully put, Adam. Encouraging others is essential. I will always remind us to extend our kindness to those around us." Bobby responded, amazed at how his son's depth unfurled, stemming from their shared insights.

As the evening lingered on, they exchanged one final promise, their voices synchronizing in harmony. "We promise to remember that we are a team!" They declared, sealing their shared aspirations with an invisible thread that bound them.

With that promise echoing through the twilight air, Adam leaned back in his chair, gazing up into the starry expanse, feeling an indescribable warmth enveloping him. The conversations they shared drifted into the night, echoing in the cosmos like a celestial chant of hope and interconnectedness.

As Bobby joined Adam in looking skyward, he whispered, "There are countless stories in the universe just waiting to be shared. Storytellers and artists make history, while we continue writing our own. As long as we nurture our bond and embrace our creativity, together we will paint a masterpiece of our lives, one promise at a time."

The cool night air settled around them, the sounds of the world winding down like a gentle lullaby. A profound sense of tranquility swept over them; the uncertainties of the future lay vast, but together, they felt fortified by the promises crafted under the watchful gaze of the stars.

In the weeks that followed, Adam and Bobby kept their promises alive. They gathered at their kitchen table, armed with colored pencils and blank sheets of paper, as they embarked on their first collaborative art night. Every stroke of color held laughter, creativity, and unyielding connection—they were co-authors of a new chapter in their lives.

During quiet mornings over pancakes, they would share dreams of places they wished to visit, mapping out distant lands on napkins. In those moments, their future transformed into a vibrant tapestry, with each promise adding a splash of color to the evolving mural of their lives.

As seasons changed, the library became a second home where they explored new stories, aligning their experiences alongside the lessons of each tale, ever mindful of their sacred commitments.

The promise of growth beckoned them to be students of each other's hearts, learning the language of vulnerability, instilled with the courage to embrace the messy beauty life presented. Adam's laughter became the melody of their household, while Bobby's art flourished once more, inspired by the moments they shared.

As they often returned to the library, armed with their list of future adventures, the world blossomed in anticipation of boundless possibilities. Every shared experience carried within it a kernel of wisdom they had both vowed to keep alive, stitching the fabric of their lives closer together.

The tangible promises, their intertwined hearts, held the key to transforming mundane moments into extraordinary memories. Each promise manifested as a thread weaving throughout the stories they shared—an ever-growing testament of love and connection rooted in kindness, creativity, and boundless exploration.

Time flowed gently, carrying them toward a horizon bright with the light of possibilities. Underneath the starry sky, Bobby and Adam continued climbing the ladder of growth together, hand-in-hand, as their journey unfurled—a journey filled with imagination, love, and the unyielding strength of promises made beneath the cosmos.

Conclusion

Thank You, Fearless Explorers!

Wow, can you believe we made it to the end? I want to take a moment, a heartfelt one, to thank you for riding this roller coaster of a narrative with me. Each page turned, each laugh shared, and every thoughtful pause has been an absolute joy. That's a win-win for both of us! You didn't just read a book; you experienced a journey intertwined with laughter, learning, and perhaps some mind-bending realizations along the way.

Reflecting back on this adventure, it's incredible to think about the questions we've danced around. We've challenged ideas and poked at norms, and I hope that spark ignited something within you, urging you to dig deeper and explore further. Remember, each conclusion in life leads us to a new beginning. The end of this book doesn't mean the end of your discoveries—it's merely a launchpad. So, launch yourself into the world with the knowledge and inspiration you've gathered here!

I'm excited for what's next in your journey! Share the insights, the giggles, and those little lightbulb moments you've experienced—it spreads the magic! You might just inspire someone else to embark on their path of inquiry and exploration. Think about it: your enthusiasm can set off a ripple effect in someone else's life. Isn't that wonderfully contagious?

As we part ways for now, but not forever, I urge you to take that wondrous energy and channel it. Challenge conventions and explore the unfamiliar! The world is bursting with opportunities for growth and wonder—dare to jump into the unknown with your eyes wide open! And if you ever find yourself bogged down or lost, don't forget to revisit the chapters here. This book is now a part of you, a companion on your journey.

So, here's to you, my fellow adventurer! Go forth with courage and curiosity—each day is written with potential for new stories waiting to unfold. Thank you once again for your time, your trust, and for weaving your unique energy into this adventure. May your path be as vibrant and unstoppable as your spirit!

With joy and endless possibilities!

Christopher Richardson.

9 781965 138823